MW00834202

THE UNSOLVED CASE OF THE SECRET CHRISTMAS BABY

A VICTORIAN COZY MYSTERY

THE MRS IMOGENE LYNCH SERIES
BOOK 1

HANNAH BYRON

Copyright © 2022 by Hannah Byron

All rights reserved.

No part of this book may be reproduced in any form or by any electronic or mechanical means, including information storage and retrieval systems, without written permission from the author, except for the use of brief quotations in a book review.

This is a work of fiction and not a history book. Names, characters, businesses, places, events, and incidents are either the products of the author's imagination or used in a fictitious manner. Even though actual facts and names have been used to serve, any resemblance to actual persons, living or dead, or actual events is purely coincidental and should be read in the context of a fictional story.

Cover designer: EbookLaunch
Editor: Michele Chiappetta of Two Bird Author Services
2nd Editor: Amber Fritz-Hewer
Website: Hannah Byron
eBook ISBN: 978-90-832156-7-9
Paperback ISBN: 978-90-832156-9-3

"*Though a good deal is too strange to be believed, nothing is too strange to have happened.*"

Thomas Hardy

NOTE TO READERS

There is no Dartmond, nor Tiversack Lake, nor
Landdulton, nor Hungry Summit Hills.
But The Cotswolds are very real, and drop-dead
charming!

OUR CAST OF DARTMOND CHARACTERS

Mrs Imogene Bowditch-Lynch the widow, new to solving murders

Chief-constable Thaddeus Lynch Imogene's *deceased* husband

Roly-Poly Jasper Imogene's Jack Russell terrier

Sir Finley Lowther the secret Christmas baby, Imogene's cousin, squire of Gladmers

Lady Anna Lynch-Lowther Finley's wife, also Thaddeus's sister

Lady Kittie Lowther Finley's assumed mother, resident of Ridgeview Asylum

Lady Catherine Lowther Finley's (half?) sister, Imogene's cousin

Mr Ephraim Galway the Landdulton solicitor, Finley's friend

Miss Eloise Platt Dartmond's unelected mayor & haberdashery owner

Mr Rahul Banerjee the new Dartmond mayor

Gertie Clubb Imogene's Dartmond maid

Emilie Pocock the schoolmaster's wife, also schoolmistress

Timothy Pocock the Pococks' son, Jasper's friend

Cornelia Hopewell the paper shop owner's wife

Richard Hopewell the paper shop owner & Imogene's landlord

Assistant Constable Axel Candy Landdulton's junior policeman

Constable Columbus Walsh Dartmond's senior policeman

Miss Theresa Philpot *The Cotswolds Times* reporter

Miss Hermine Tow the post office mistress

Mary Huckstep the baker's wife

Rosamond Suthmeer the doctor's wife

Edmund Suthmeer Dartmond's medical doctor

Minnie Fritter the fishmonger's wife

Donald Fritter the fishmonger

Neil Fritter the Fritters' eldest son, Gertie's love interest

Alfie Fritter the Fritters' youngest son

Hardy Crowle Mr Banerjee's assistant

PROLOGUE

Landdulton, January 1895

It is a crisp and frosty morning in early January when Sir Finley Lowther, with a swift gait despite his considerable weight, makes his way up the steps to a glass-panelled door that reads *Messrs Ephraim Galway & Lambert Watson, Solicitors* in ornate, golden lettering. The expression on his broad face, with a well-coiffed moustache and ocean grey eyes, is serious, perhaps even somewhat morose. A visit to one's solicitor is hardly ever a joy.

Taking a moment to catch his breath, he retrieves his golden snuffbox from the pocket of his waistcoat, which is a well-cut garment of excellent quality wool in a pattern of black and white lozenges. The white of the waistcoat is the only exception to his overall, black mourning attire. Finley is in mourning for his father, Sir Reginald Lowther, who passed away peacefully on the first of January.

Sir Finley stops at the top of the steps to take a pinch of the ground tobacco between his stubby fingers, which he pops routinely behind his full underlip. Deftly slipping the box back in place, he pushes the door open with visibly more pep.

The spacious hall with the tiled floor and high, painted ceiling is agreeably warm on this wintry day. Sir Finley presses his card into the waiting bellboy's hand and hangs his overcoat and top hat on the coat rack.

Minutes later, the newly-promoted Squire of Landdulton is seated in one of Mr Galway's mahogany-brown Chesterfield armchairs, crossing his legs in their black trousers, smoothing the creases. Opposite him is seated his long-time friend and hunting partner, Ephraim Galway, with a sympathetic look on his elongated, white face with thin nose and shrewd black eyes. The solicitor seems set on cheering up his best friend but goes about it in the opposite way.

"What a rigmarole your father's will is, Fin. Who'd have thought you might not be a Lowther by birth? Well, you always be one to me, dear friend. Whatever the outcome of Sir Reginald's preposterous claims." The solicitor taps the tips of his slender fingers together making the diamond in his signet ring flash in the electric light.

Finley shifts in his chair, thunderclouds forming in his grey eyes. "What nonsense are you talking, Efry? For sure, you knew of this change to my father's will!" He looks sour, drops his chewing tobacco in the ashtray and lights a cigar. Then starts puffing on it without offering one to his friend. Ephraim throws his thin arms in the air in protest.

"What distrust, my dear fellow. Have I ever lied to you? Or deceived you? Right after your father apparently told you about your adoption, he ordered me to Gladmers Manor to change his will. He told me you knew about the change but that I had to wait for *your* visit *to* me. I was ordered to maintain complete confidentiality. So that's what I did."

The hands go up again, this time as giving himself over to the power of the late Sir Reginald. Finley hesitates, seems to weigh his friend's words against his own experience, then frowns once more.

"All right. Don't work yourself up, Efry. It's quite enough for one of us to be in a pickle."

"You're not in a pickle by any measure, Fin. I know a way around this if you want."

That seems to perk up the squire to some extent.

"Well, you'll have to tell me what's in the will before I can decide on that."

Now it's Ephraim's turn to pause.

"What do you know, Fin? What exactly did your father tell you? As you can understand, he gave me no details about your birth or this presumed adoption. Just told me to add the clause that it's your duty to find the biological mother and give her ten percent of the inheritance. If you fail to find her, that ten percent has to be given to the Foundling Hospital in Bristol." Here, the solicitor shows his face. "Note, *if* you fail to find her, you can pay that hospital anonymously, and nobody will ever find out you may have been compromised in some sort of scandal."

"Get me a brandy first. I hear my father's voice again, telling me that exact thing. I hate talking about this business. It upsets me. Not to talk about how much it's upsetting Anna as well."

The solicitor nods, rings the bell, and the liquor is served in a wink by the bellboy.

"Terrible business all around for you and your wife. I don't understand why your father deemed it necessary to confess this adoption history on his deathbed."

"Oh, he wanted to die with a clean conscience," Finley observes, sipping his drink. "You know how my father was. A lot of wool-gathering and mystifications, but when it came to the crunch, he wanted to die with a clear conscience about what he'd done. And amend for it in his own way."

"So, what *did* he do?" The solicitor is getting impatient, leaving his own drink untouched.

Finley smiles a thin smile. "I wish I knew. The desire for mystifications never completely evaporated. But apparently my insane mother, you know Lady Lowther, who's been in Ridgeview Asylum for decades and is never talked about by the family anymore, is not my biological mother. She only had my sister Catherine, but where I exactly came from and whether my father is my biological father, he didn't want to disclose for privacy of the biological mother. Can you imagine?" Finley's eyes get the turbulent ocean quality again.   "He *knew*, but he wouldn't tell me. Just barked at me to get Constable Lynch involved as he's my brother-in-law and has access to archives that might help find the mother. Have you ever heard of such nonsense? And you know what is the rottenest thing of all? My father seemed to know where to find this woman, but he clearly wanted to saddle me with his last mystery. Well, he liked those things. I don't."

Finley is fuming with anger now while Ephraim looks pensive.

"Think of it this way. Your father might have had a good reason not to disclose the woman's identity. Have you considered asking Lady Lowther herself?"

Finley sits up straighter, still angry. "Are you mad, Efry? No one goes to Ridgeview Asylum. She's not been seen since I was born. I don't even know her. And I have no longing to change that."

Ephraim sits back in his chair, the fingertip-touching starting again. "But your brother-in-law is terribly ill himself. How can he undertake such a case now?"

"Exactly!" the squire exclaims, finishing his drink and banging the crystal glass back on the ivory tray. "I don't want Thaddeus to break his head over it, but it's too late. Anna apparently told Imogene and Thaddeus is now frantically trying to get the evidence together by going into the archives of what happened at Christmas in 1845, when I was born."

"Imogene, being your cousin, just wants to help you," the solicitor offers.

"Yes, of course she does. And that's all well and good, my entire family getting involved, but I'm not sure I want to rake up this old history. It's not like I'm suddenly bereft with no mother in my life - I haven't had a mother, biological or adopted for 50 years." Finley looks gloomy.

"Is it perhaps the inheritance you don't want to share?" The solicitor's dark eyes rest on his friend.

"God, man, no. That's the least of my concern. It's not like I'll be a pauper if I give away some of my money. It's this emotional thing I hate - digging up scandal and drama when it is all decades old and serves no purpose."

It is silent in the solicitor's office for a while. Finley puffs on his cigar and Ephraim studies his fingernails.

"So, what will you do now?" The solicitor is the first to speak. "I told you that you can pretend to attempt to find her and then just pay the money to the Foundling Hospital?"

"And I told *you* I don't care about the money." Finley snaps, easing himself out of the deep chair. "Let me think about it. I came here hoping you knew more about this mess, but apparently you only got the will. Finley pauses, and lets out a deep sigh, "It's all right, Efry, really it is. I'll sort this out myself and will let you know one way or the other."

Ephraim rises to his full length as well, a frown in between his eyes. "I'm so sorry for all this, Fin. Certainly so soon after your father's passing and with your brother-in-law being so ill. You're going through a rough period. Will you be at the Club this Thursday?"

The men shake hands, still the best of friends.

"Of course, the Club's the only bright spot in my miserable existence right now. See you for a proper game of billiards on Thursday night, and make sure you let me win to improve my mood."

"Done deal, friend. All the best."

PART I

CASE UNSOLVED

1

WHY I MOVED TO DARTMOND AND MUCH MORE

Dartmond, 21 December 1895

I honest to goodness wish I'd never made this promise to my late husband, but I have. And now I must suffer the consequences, as sure as that a man shaved has lost his beard. While Christmas descends upon us once again with tinsel, holly, and sweet-toned carols, I'm sitting here in my alcove chair peering through lace curtains, wondering how to bring this fifty-year-old mystery to a good end. A business almost as old as I am myself.

One thing is as sure as eggs and bacon, and that's that this whole Christmas baby mystery is a thorn in my flesh. Though my dear Thaddeus used to discuss his cases with me in his function as Landdulton's chief constable, I've never heard him talk of having to solve an adoption. It really doesn't sound like something the police need to get involved in, now does it?

Well, here's the thing. It isn't a case in the traditional

sense. Thaddeus wanted to have it cleared because it concerns our family. And to be honest, his illness also made him so frantic about solving it before he passed, and why he made me promise, nay swear, I'd solve it in his place.

This folder I'm holding here probably concerns some secret adoption involving my cousin Finley, newly inherited Squire of Gladder Manor. So quite a delicate matter all around. Also, with two miscarriages of my own, quite some years ago, everything revolving around infants and parenthood is precarious to me. My Thaddeus and I had long resigned ourselves to our childless state and took a dog instead. Now, with my blessed one gone, my benedict, as they say, my roly-poly Jasper is all I have. Just look at him there. Fast asleep like an angel, snoring and passing gas with all four paws stretched out on his red-velvet throne. Such a sweetheart.

But let's get back to why Jasper and I are here in Dartmond in the first place. In a town where I'm a stranger, without my husband to count on, and away from my lovely home, Honeydew Mansion in Landdulton.

My home may be only twenty miles down the road, but it feels as far away as Africa to me. When Thaddeus started his investigation in January of this year, partially on the request of Finley, my cousin and partially on the request of Finley's wife Anna and Thaddeus's sister, he certainly hoped to finish it himself, but he was already way too ill then. He should never have considered embarking on such an emotional endeavour.

The long and the short of it is, that my benedict left us on 17 April of this year. But let's not go there. It upsets me so.

I knew why solving this mystery was so important to him. He wanted to leave, having found peace for his family, but alas, God didn't grant him the time. That's why it is on me now to find the answers for him. Even more so than for Finley, who usually shrugs it off when I try to discuss it with him.

"Thaddeus Lynch," I say to myself every morning on waking up, "couldn't you have given me an easier burden to carry?"

I miss my house and my domestic routines, being cooped up here in rented accommodation that has seen better times, but I'm not sure I'd be able to face living alone in my lovely abode without my better half.

So, I hang in between two worlds, keeping tabs on a woman across the street from me who could have something to do with Finley's adoption.

BUT BEFORE WE go further into the details about her, let me introduce myself. I'm Mrs Imogene Lynch, a new widow who's about to turn forty-nine on 25 December. I share my unusual birthdate with my cousin Finley, who, until his father's deathbed announcement, had no idea he had been adopted at birth fifty years earlier.

You might assume I love Christmas because of my birthday, but this year I'm not looking forward to it. I am missing Thaddeus even more than usual. It will be so silent, just Jasper and me, but I've promised myself I will attend Midnight Mass at Trinity Church here in Dartmond, if only to show I'm trying to be a social being.

Mourning does that to a person, you just want to be left alone, stewing in your misery.

So far, though, the Christmas season hasn't been too bad. I enjoy watching the folks' comings and goings on Darren Street from my first-floor window. Hardly a dull moment. Despite the biting wind and this year's early snowfall, Dartmonders still go out to socialise and do their shopping.

My own preparations for Christmas are already done. Gertie, my new maid, will poke up the fire in the morning room, where I'll seat myself at my small round table for one. As I'm still in mourning, I'll wear my usual black taffeta dress with a freshly starched lace collar. I call it my Queen Victoria uniform, though I look nothing like her.

Thin as a rail, Thaddeus used to say, but he meant it as a compliment. I'd preferred 'willowy' but never told him. I like that word. As if my roots are planted solidly, but the rest of me waves in the wind. Anyway, no trout or turkey for me. A slice of cooked ham, boiled potatoes–*teddies* they call them here–and two serving spoons of winter cabbage. That will do for me. I'm not frugal. I just have little of an appetite.

As I sit here at my window, pondering my widowed state, I know quite well that not long after Christmas, it will be time for me to break some ground with my prime "suspect" in this adoption investigation. It's not that I've been twiddling my thumbs the past nine months; it's just that it took Jasper and me much more time than I expected to grow accustomed to living in these cramped quarters over a bookshop in the middle of a busy, unfamiliar town.

After the luxury of our wonderful Honeydew

Mansion overlooking Tiversack Lake, any other place would look like a dump.

I can hear you think, if Mrs Lynch was accustomed to the good life, why didn't she get herself a proper place in Dartmond? It's a fair question to which I can give you a straightforward answer. I need to be where I can keep an eye on Miss Platt's haberdasher shop and observe the Dartmond people she acquaints herself with. How else can I investigate any irregularities regarding my candidate as Finley's birth mother?

So, I live here with Gertie Clubb, who's quite a handful and much more work for me than my loyal housekeeper of twenty-five years, Mrs Peaton, ever was. Oh, the girl thinks I don't pay attention to her fluffing a bit of dust here and there so she can skip across the road to the post office and gossip with the postmistress, Hermine Tow. I'm also not sure Gertie wouldn't snoop in my papers, so I make sure I lock my secretaire and keep the key in my dress pocket.

Not a bad girl, just somewhat lazy and nosy. Regularly sleeps through the knocker-upper I pay a pence a month to wake her up at 6.00 a.m. by knocking on her window with his pole. If she sleeps in, I get out of bed without the fire being lit. And I can tell you that's as unpleasurable as ice-water in your shoe.

"HELLO, Jasper, are you done napping, my dear?"

He's opening one drowsy eyelid. Ah, his belly is waking him. The old thing eats almost more than I do. Well, it shows, I guess. My Roly-Poly can't get down these narrow stairs by himself anymore. Gertie must carry him in her arms, which she hates. But what am I to do about the poor thing's weight?

"Come here, Jasper darling. I'll ring the bell cord and ask Gertie to bring you your jellied meat."

I watch with an ache in my heart at how slowly he gets to his feet. Arthritis. He ambles over to my chair, dragging his belly over the floor. It's so hard to see him getting stiffer by the day, especially in this winter cold. I can't part with him, not now.

As I pat his white-and-tan head, he collapses at my feet with a deep doggie sigh, his snout on my shoe. I ring the bell, half expecting not to get a response. Gertie can be so sluggish.

I would love to get up myself and stretch but I'm sitting put, waiting for the Miss-Platt-morning-ceremony. Ah, I hear Gertie coming. When will she lift her feet instead of dragging them? Who brought her up? I was told she lived in an orphanage until she was sixteen, and clearly no one had the time to teach gracefulness to the young women. Gertie has had one other house before she came to me, and apparently they didn't manage to lighten her steps at all. Now she's here with me and sleeps in the small alcove next to the kitchen and tromps all over the flat.

"You called, Ma'am?" Pronouncing her l's as w's, a typically west-country accent. I'm accustomed to the dialect by now, having lived away from London for over thirty years.

Gertie is certainly not a bad-looking girl with her slanted eyes, a kind of greyish-green colour that changes from morning to night. Her hair, a sort of middle brown, could do with a good brushing out. A bit on the chubby side, but she still may grow out of that early fat. And at least her apron is clean today and there's no soot under her nails. I nod, smiling my special, Gertie smile, which shows my willingness to have patience with her.

"Yes, I rang for you, Gertie." I gaze at the watch around my neck as if to say, *you should have been here fifteen minutes ago.* I've told her the routine over and over and yet she forgets it. Deliberately or not, I do not know.

At times like this, I dearly miss Mrs Peaton, who stayed behind to run Honeydew Mansion in my absence.

"Time to prepare Jasper's breakfast."

My dear one lifts his head at my voice, and a red tongue licks his blubbery lips.

"Right on, Ma'am. You want me to take him dreckly to the kitchen, or will you feed him yourself?" Gertie replies, deftly skipping every h in the sentence.

"You take him *directly*, Gertie." I could start by teaching her proper English. "And please bring me a fresh pot of tea. This one's cold."

"Coming, Ma'am. Anything else you wanted?"

"That'll do, Gertie. Just make sure you take the wee one outside to do his business before you bring him back in here."

"Alrite, Ma'am."

Jasper hobbles on his short legs after the maid. I exhale after she closes the door.

Be strict with staff on day one, Imogene, or they'll outfox you on day two. That's my dear Mama's voice. Well, I never had reason to be strict with Mrs Peaton. It was rather the other way around. She knew everything the way it was supposed to be done. Much better than I did, having never immersed myself in the managing of my parents' home in Kensington. Mother was so good at these things.

While I'm waiting for my fresh Darjeeling tea, I return to my vigilance at the window. What was I telling you when Jasper woke? Oh yes, I was complaining about my narrow sitting room, the tiny kitchen and two bedrooms that can hardly fit a sizable bed. Mould and dust are included in the price of 50p rent a week.

Used as I was to living in a spacious house in central London and then in the gorgeous thatched-roofed villa Thaddeus bought for us outside Landdulton, I'm out of sorts here.

It's just for the duration of the investigation, Imogene, I repeat to myself every day, as I focus on what happens outside, not inside. I need this place more than it needs me. It just gives me the discretion and privacy I need to spy on the town until I solve this mystery.

FIVE MORE MINUTES until Miss Platt's arrival.

THERE'S OUR MISS PLATT FOR YOU

While we wait for our key player to arrive on the scene, let me tell you what I've found out about her so far. Apparently, Miss Eloise Platt is the most well-respected spinster in all Dartmond. Though from the way she looks, you'd never have gathered that Miss Eloise, as everyone calls her, was an influential Dartmonder.

The grey-haired, tightly bunned, stringy sixty-six-year-old has been a resident of this small town all her life. Dartmond lies tucked between Hungry Summit Hills and Tiversack Lake in the middle of the Cotswolds. It has some fifteen hundred souls in total. Just a pinprick on the world's map, but one that's dear to Miss Eloise, whom I'll refer to as Miss Platt.

Our Miss Platt owns her own cottage - a lacklustre, grey limestone dwelling on the fringe of Dartmond - next to the outbound road, Lakeside Path, that runs along the lake to the neighbouring Landdulton. However, she spends most of her time in her haberdashery called *Trea-*

sures and Trinkets, here on Darren Street, right across from me.

I'm located halfway down Darren Street, Dartmond's main street. This way I can see all the comings and goings left and right of me. Thaddeus would've agreed it is the perfect perch from which to watch all activity, though he'd be appalled at my current living conditions.

Miss Platt inherited the haberdashery from her parents. That's what I understood from Thaddeus's notes. When she temporarily went missing as a sixteen-year-old girl in 1845, the Platts owned the shop right where it is now and lived above it. I don't know when she bought the cottage and stopped living over the shop. Maybe it held poor memories for her.

I also don't know what happened to Miss Platt's sister, Mrs Beatrice Platt-Jones. She's mentioned as married in 1845 in *The Cotswolds Times'* article. But where she went and why, I haven't found out. Probably just moved away from Dartmond.

Though I like puzzles and guesses, I can't figure Miss Platt out from what I've read about her. And I miss Thaddeus so much when my mind gets blurry like this, and I can't concentrate. He would've told me what hints to look for. After all, he was the best constable in the entire district. Well, there's no crying over spilt milk. It's my job to find out as much as I can about this unreadable woman.

As far as Miss Platt's clientele at her haberdashery goes, I don't see many customers go into the shop, which makes me wonder how she gets by. Sometimes my charitable side plays up and I think of crossing the street to purchase some unnecessary lace or buttons from her.

The amount of charity work Miss Platt does herself is astounding. When she's not tottering around her knitting needles, buttons, and yards of English lace, she seems to chair the Dartmond Ladies Reader Society, or organise the Saint Mary's Primary School charities, or heading the Trinity Church Flower Arrangement Group. Heaven knows why, as she certainly doesn't look like a society-loving woman.

The doctor's wife, Mrs Suthmeer, told me people in Dartmond have taken to calling Miss Platt their unelected mayor. That's where my brain gets muddled. This inconspicuous creature effectively *runs* the town. And for some reason, Dartmond doesn't have a real mayor.

These past weeks have been all about Miss Platt's Dartmond Christmas Decoration Committee. Her long navy-blue skirts sweeping through slush and snow, and in her faded blue coat, she pointed out with long, tapered fingers where the gas lamps needed to go, where the strings of holly and tinsel had to be hung. She didn't go up the ladder herself, but she looked like she wanted to. Tireless creature, not a lazy bone in her body.

I've been watching all this Miss Platt activity happen before my eyes with interest. There's a grim tenacity in the woman, a will to survive any odds and perhaps also to be seen and heard. But there's still an odd discrepancy between her position and how unassuming she is, like she doesn't care for people around her, but seeks them out all the time against her will. Odd kettle of fish, for sure.

Speaking of a low profile, that's what I keep here myself for obvious reasons. Go to church on Sundays, with my eyes kept open, unless we're praying. Sometimes I do my own shopping to mingle among the townsfolk. I'm sure they think I'm an odd kettle of fish myself with my London accent and refined mourning clothes.

Dartmonders are less refined than Landdultoners. I don't want them to think I feel above them because I don't. I can't help the way I sound. In Landdulton, folk were used to my way of speaking and respected me because of my husband, but here I'm not so sure what they make of me.

FINALLY, it is 9 o'clock sharp. You must be tired of me elaborating on my observations.

Here's our Miss Platt coming onto the scene. She's rolling her rusty bike with its peeled-off blue paint past Herby's grocery shop around the corner of Darren Street. Why she doesn't ride the old thing but pushes it around, only heaven knows. I've never seen her ride it. Maybe it's broken.

She moves underneath the red and green tinsels that her Dartmond Christmas Decoration Committee hung along the street. A frosty wind whirls them around. She plods on stoically to her shop, where I fear she'll see few customers today. All the Christmas attire has been bought and nobody sews at Christmas time.

When there are no other people around, she's so closed into herself. A sad soul moving along in her faded blue raincoat that has seen too many seasons and is too thin for this weather. It's at least three sizes too big. Either she's lost weight over the years, or it's just her dress style.

I've never seen her wear another coat since my arrival in April.

The hem of a long navy skirt, every day the same one, touches her worn-out, flat, brown shoes that seem to hasten by the side of the bike. Is she speeding up as she passes my house? I glance at the face with the thin gold-rimmed spectacles that hide her tired blue eyes. Now she crosses the street and parks the bike in front of it.

She takes the key from her coat's wide pocket and enters the darkness of *Treasures and Trinkets*. Miss Platt is here to face another day.

Time for me to get up and stretch. I've got a job lain out for me.

"Now stop whining, Gertie, and just walk slowly down the stairs. Jasper isn't even 2 stone. You carry heavier sacks of potatoes up the stairs."

"But I carry the teddies up the stairs, Ma'am, not down. He is heavier than a three-year-old babber."

A three-year-old baby? Have you ever heard of such an exaggeration? One day soon, that maid's going to do me in. She shuffles down the stairs so slowly, I'm almost losing my balance, and mind you, these stairs are as narrow as a rabbit hole.

"Just hold him steady, will you, or you'll scare him, and you know what happens then!"

But it's too late. Jasper whimpers once, and the damage is done.

"Ma'am, he's wee-weeing all over me dress."

"Poor darling Jasper, we'll sort you out downstairs.

Don't squeeze him so tight, Gertie, I told you a dozen times before. It frightens him. And keep moving now. You can change your dress in a minute."

Dear Lord in Heaven, what is it with this maid? I can't go through this every time with her and the dog.

When we finally land in one piece on the mat in the tight hallway near the glass-panelled front door, she puts poor Jasper on all fours. He looks up at me with those large, guilt-ridden eyes, but the stricken soul can't help this. Enough is enough.

"It's all right, Jasper dear. Gertie, I'll ask if Neil Fritter wants to earn a little extra pocket money and carry Jasper up and down, all right? We can't have you change dresses three times a day."

"That's gurt lush, Ma'am."

"Nice of me? Well, it's all right, Gertie. Now change and wash that dress. I'll pop into Donald's fish shop on my way back and see if Neil is available."

"And I'm sorry for the mess, Ma'am."

Don't think that I miss the flicker of hope in Gertie's grey eyes. Yes, Neil Fritter is a bit of a looker, so she won't mind seeing him upstairs. I'll make sure he delivers Jasper at my front door and doesn't come in. I'm not against romancing, but I'll not encourage it either in un-betrothed people. That's not my style.

When the buttons of Jasper's red-checked duffel coat are all done up, I take the leash from the bewildered Gertie.

"Now, now, dear, there are worse calamities in the world. Don't you fret no more."

I can't be strict with people when they're looking at me like this. No matter that my mother's voice is nagging me. "And have a cup of tea and a slice of shortbread."

"Thank you, Ma'am. I will." The gritty smile I get tells me I've done the right thing.

"Come on, Jasper sweet, we are going to brace the cold."

And with that, I step into Darren Street and inhale the frosty air. It smells of peat fires, mulled wine and caramelized apples. When we pass Huckstep Bakery, the sugary, spiced smell of mince-pies wafts into my nose. Jasper's nozzle registers it too and his tail perks up.

"On our way back, my little gourmand!" I promise him, as I enjoy being out of doors after that stagnant morning with my own conundrums. Ah, there's Mrs Pocock with her son, Timothy. What a sweet face she has under that frilly bonnet. Such a pretty thing. Think the boy takes more after his father. A bit solemn and too skinny.

"Hello dear, enjoying a break from the schoolroom?" I might as well invite her for a chat. Have a longer look at those pretty, long eyelashes and that fine mouth. Wonder if she's from the West country. Hardly an accent in her clear voice.

"Hello, Mrs Lynch. Yes, it's wonderful to just be the mistress of the house for once. Hello, Jasper. Can Timothy stroke him?"

"Of course! Jasper loves all attention."

"Would you care to come for a cup of tea one of these days, Mrs Lynch? It must be quite lonely here on your own at this time of year."

Ah, there's at least one Dartmonder who's got her eyes open. I smile at her.

"That would be delightful, but you will be so busy with visitors." I try to fend such a direct invitation off with ingrained politeness.

"No, not at all. My folk are all in Kent and don't travel at this time of year and Mr Pocock, unfortunately, doesn't have any family anymore, so it's just the three of us."

Timothy is sitting on his haunches caressing Jasper's soft ears, and the two of them seem to form an instant bond.

I hesitate. I'm not sure I'm ready for social calls, yet the prospect of spending the long Christmas days on my own looks quite bleak. But I declined Finley's and Anna's open invitation to go down to Gladmers Manor this year. It simply isn't done to go over to strangers but did not sit with my family.

After all, it's both Finley's and my birthday. The Lowthers understood, though, that on this first Christmas without Thaddeus, I need some privacy. Mrs Pocock must have observed my deliberation.

"I'm sorry, Mrs Lynch. I shouldn't have invited you like this. I know you're still in mourning. Please forgive me."

I shake myself from my thoughts. What am I trying to achieve here? I'll visit Finley and Anna for New Year's Day. It will give me an opportunity to go through all the details of what he knows in relation to his adoption. So, I hear myself say bluntly:

"No, it's all right. It's a delightful suggestion and will take me out of my misanthropy."

"Will you bring Jasper, Mrs Lynch?" Two marble-round, brown eyes look up at me and I see the resemblance to Timothy's mother now. Same features, after all. Only the hair is like his father's.

"Would you like that, Timothy? I don't know if your parents agree to dogs inside the house?"

"Oh yes, no problem at all. So would Boxing Day suit you, say, at three 'o'clock?" Mrs Pocock is not doing this just out of politeness. She is really inviting me to her house.

I nod, smile, bid them good day. Jasper gets his last pat from a small white hand. There is a new lightness in our step as we continue our way.

Have I been that lonesome? I haven't even noticed I was in the doldrums, being so totally cooped up inside my own thoughts. The brief chat with Mrs Pocock warmed my heart and makes me temporarily bold, so I cross the road after looking left and right. If I don't do it now, I probably will never.

Miss Platt's rusty bicycle with the peeled-off blue paint stands against the front of *Treasures and Trinkets*. The shop's facade could also benefit from a lick of paint. Jasper's pulling his leash. He has no interest in haberdashery, but more in the fish shop next door.

"One moment, Jasper dear. Let me check out this Cluny lace. Life revolves not only around your roly-poly stomach."

He's such an obedient dog, sits on his behind on the freezing pavement with the tips of his ears hanging. I inspect the shop windows and instantly observe it lacks all the wear-and-tear of the outside. Miss Platt's articles are displayed in a neat and attractive manner. Needles, threads, lace, buttons, ribbons in the left window, knitting wool and finished examples in the middle one, and men's suits, shirts, and neckties in the right window.

She has displayed everything against a backdrop of deep-red velvet and sprinkled the velvet with bits of holly and pinecones to give it a Christmas feeling. One thing is clear as crystal to me, Miss Platt cares a great deal for her shop.

I make a job of studying the left window, as I abhor knitting–the sound of these clicking needles is enough to make me jittery–and I have no need for a new man's suit. Mind you, all Thaddeus's clothes are still in the big mahogany cupboard at Honeydew Mansion, with plenty of cedar balls against the moths. I haven't been able to part with that personal legacy yet. His shirts still smell of tobacco and eau de cologne. But none of that now.

Lace? Do I need more lace? Probably not, but a lady can never have enough lace. Miss Platt's Bedfordshire lace is good quality. Her Brussels Needlepoint lace is a bit yellow at the edges, but I particularly like her Cluny lace. It's excellent guipure, bobbin lace. It would go well with the lavender dress I've ordered for the new year when I go into half-mourning.

While I peer through the old, grooved window to get a better look at the lace, I'm aware of a pair of eyes keeping tabs on me from inside the shop. The whites of the eyes stand out in the dusky recesses.

She's watching me like I watch her from behind the gauze curtains of my apartment.

Well, you have a good look, Miss Platt, as you'll probably see a lot more of me in the foreseeable future.

And to myself I say, "Spin the bottle, Imogene, are you going in, or are you going to be a ninny?"

The moment I need to make up my mind or make a fool of myself from staring at Miss Platt's shop windows for too long, I see the buxom Rosamond Suthmeer, the doctor's wife, cross the street. She walks with these quick, dainty steps, very contrary to her portly figure. I suppose she's imitating that hoity-toity industrialist's wife, Winnifred Herriot, who's a bit of a celebrity here in town and wears such tight skirts around her ankles and high-heeled boots, she can't move her legs properly.

Mrs Suthmeer has that do-or-die expression on her round face, plus a big smile, most likely directed at my address.

"Ah, Mrs Lynch, so good to see you out and about. Were you considering buying some ribbons, or perhaps lace? I absolutely must get myself some of that gorgeous Brussels Needlepoint. It's the latest fashion, isn't it?"

Jasper snarls at my feet, and I hush him. I wish the dear one wasn't so sensitive to my likes and dislikes, but he is.

But this time, I see Rosamond's intervention as a blessing.

"Ah, Mrs Suthmeer, yes, I agree, lovely lace. Were you going inside?"

"Yes, let's go together and give Miss Platt some customers to attend to." She grabs my elbow, which results in another snarl from Jasper, which I stop.

It's the first time I step into this rather dusky-looking shop, but I'm immediately struck at the way it smells. Scent is important to me. It's rather refreshing–camphor, lavender, leather wax. The shop's size is also remarkable, well-carpeted and spacious. One wouldn't have fathomed that from outside.

Again, that division in three—three counters, three departments: small haberdasher items, knitting, and men's clothing. Miss Platt rises from an old armchair where she was sitting, knitting what looks like a green jumper with white intarsia patterns. A small boy's size.

Her blue dress is quite pretty and doesn't look as sloven as I had expected. She's changed into new shoes as well.

After pushing her spectacles higher on the bridge of her thin nose, her hands go instinctively to her grey hair, patting it as if it is out of form. I'm glad for Rosamond to speak first.

"I brought you a new customer, Eloise. Have you met Mrs Lynch?"

We look at each other, take each other's measurement. This is an intelligent woman opposite me, tired and worn-down, but sharp as a freshly filed pencil.

"Please to meet you." I stretch out my hand and she shakes it. The hand is bony and warm, the wool of her half-mittened fingers tickle the inside of my hand.

"I haven't. It's a pleasure to meet you, Mrs Lynch." The voice is firm. I hear years of chairing groups and ordering supplies.

"Pleased to meet you, too. No objection to a dog in your shop?" She looks down at Jasper as if he's a creature from the moon, but maybe she's only surprised at his slight portliness.

"No, not at all. What can I help you ladies with?" Practised, no emotion showing on her face, though she constantly keeps me in the corner of her eyes, as I do her while she moves to her haberdashery counter. Shrewd woman, not unfriendly, difficult to gauge.

Mrs Suthmeer is practically jumping up and down at my side and blurts out, "Have you heard the latest news, Eloise? I can't believe it." The doctor's wife shakes her chubby cheeks. She's clearly not come into the shop to buy lace but to share the latest gossip.

And I must bear witness to it. If only you knew how I despise gossip. My dear late Papa's favourite quote by the Greek philosopher Socrates comes to mind. *Strong minds discuss ideas, average minds discuss events, weak minds discuss people.* That's the bread and butter I was raised on. I can see Miss Platt is mildly interested.

"What is it, Rosamond? You clearly can't wait to tell me." The bony, partially-mittened hands lay out the different lace on the counter as if she'd listened to our conversation outside. Maybe she has.

I register the women are addressing each other by their Christian names. Meaning they go back a long time and don't bother with formalities even when strangers like me are around. Duly noted.

"Oh Eloise, you mustn't take offense. Promise you won't?"

"How can I promise you anything when I do not know what you're hinting at, Rosamond?" Miss Platt continues to stoically flatten the delicate lace, but gives me a quick glance as if to see on which side I am. I have no clue.

"There's talk of a new mayor coming soon! Well, it was about time Dartmond had a proper mayor, not that you did a poor job, but this... this... is unheard of!" Mrs Suthmeer's jittery jumping increases and is further expanded by indignant snorting.

"You mean Rahul Banerjee, the son of Queen Victoria's confidant, Dr Manas Banerjee?"

Miss Platt only slightly raises one eyebrow, while her mouth curls in an ironic smile. Mrs Suthmeer seems to dislike that Miss Platt doesn't immediately support her in her disapproval of a possible Indian mayor, as she sits her voluminous behind on one chair. I smile, noticing how Miss Platt has taken the wind out of Mrs Suthmeer's little tidbit.

Looking from one to the other, I must admit Miss Platt is the one here to show all the fortitude. Even I am short of breath. An Indian mayor in the Cotswolds? Not even London is that modern. It will bring a lot of hullabaloo, that's for sure.

"I actually met Mr Rahul Banerjee yesterday," Miss Platt continues, still stroking her lace. "His father made his fortune trading in indigo, opium, and cotton before settling in Windsor and marrying an English lady. Ah well, Rahul seems a nice man. Quite like us, I would say. Agreed to those of us breaking our tongue over his name, to call him Mr Raoul Benergy. For some that might be easier." Miss Platt sniffs as if to say, 'unnecessary for me'.

But Mrs Suthmeer starts groaning like a dying horse, which upsets Jasper, who starts howling in his high-pitched boo-oooh-ooh.

"Time for a cup of tea," Miss Platt announces like a general overseeing the battlefield. I sit down on the chair next to Mrs Suthmeer and pat Jasper's head.

"That would be nice," I answer with a strange shrillness to my voice. I remind myself why I'm here, but the roles seem reversed now. Miss Platt runs the show in perfect control as she pours first the milk into three cups, adds two spoons of sugar to each, and then opens the floral tea cosy to top the cups up with steaming tea. It smells like Assam. I'm not keen on its strong malty flavour, but it will do its job under the circumstances.

When we all have our calming cup, she continues her update.

"I think we will survive a half-Indian mayor. After all, Mr Banerjee is an Oxford alumnus, and he's been brought up in England since he was a small boy. He assured me he wants to work together with the community and not overturn any apple carts. Do you like this tea, Mrs Lynch? Mr Banerjee brought it with him from his last trip to Assam. Increases mental alertness and prevents cancer in the lungs, according to him."

And not without a touch of jesting, she adds, "We need the first and pray for prevention of the last."

Then she pauses; the jest disappears as she locks her eyes with mine. For a moment there is a certain fierceness in the blue gaze, and I grit my teeth. I get the eerie feeling she knows exactly why I'm here. That I have had access to files mentioning her name.

The woman is certainly not what I expected. She's going to make my mission as impossible as counting the waves in the sea. Oh Thaddeus, what have you asked from me? But the answer is right before me.

She knows who I am and what I'm after, and I have a feeling she will cover up the truth with her life. Either she breaks or I do.

But I can't break. I made a promise.

But I'll still buy her Cluny lace. Why not? I have no use for it right now, but I'm sure it will come in handy one day.

3

GIVING THADDEUS'S CLIPPINGS
ANOTHER GOING-OVER

Back home, perked up by the chats, and, of course, the courage to meet Miss Platt, I'm sipping my tea with Jasper lying contentedly on his throne. It started snowing again, so no reason to put off the work any longer. Time to read through the newsletter clippings I found in Thaddeus's brown file.

He labelled the file *The Secret Christmas Baby* and in brackets he's written underneath in his characteristically spidery hand: *Case Unsolved*. The exterior cover of the file is full of the usual brown coffee stains. To tell you the truth, the stains move me more than the revelations in these clippings ever could.

"Why are your crime files all that drab-brown and stained?" I once asked my benedict when I brought him his afternoon coffee in his study. "One gets melancholic as a hearse plume just looking at those poor files."

He'd looked up at me from his writing, greyish-blue eyes probing me over his reading spectacles, clearly not understanding what in the world I was talking about, then smiled as he got my question. The whirly ends of his moustache lifted in a funny way when he answered, "Clearly, my dear, because these files are best at taking the coffee stains."

It was just one of these moments. Why I loved him. And my heart aches so much. He could switch quickly, my Thaddeus, and I always felt heard. That's why I have to solve this adoption situation for him, as a final 'I love you.'

This afternoon when the snow ceases, I'll go downstairs to the Hopewell's bookshop and buy myself a new red folder. I feel I've got to give this case my own swirl to solve it. After all, I don't drink coffee and I'm way less sloppy than my husband was.

Still, I dread this file and am easily distracted by seeing young Timothy Pocock again, slipping and sliding towards Huckstep's Bakery in his navy-duffel coat. Blond tuffs of hair stick from under his hood. He's such a skin-and-bones child, but I like him. Any human being that likes Jasper has already earned a place in my heart.

I know Timothy secretly goes to the bakery without his parents' permission because he can get a biscuit or a jam cake that has fallen next to the oven. "The boy's got such a sweet tooth," Mrs Huckstep told me when I got my half loaf of yeast bread. Probably another reason he and Jasper like each other. Jasper also lives for the sound of the biscuit tin being opened.

But Thaddeus calls me. I hear him loud and clear. It's almost eleven o'clock. Coffee break is over. He was a man of the clock, a constable through-and-through. I was nothing near a detective, though my benedict told me often that I would make a good one. I don't agree with him there, and that's part of my current problem. After I've delivered on this promise, I'll go back to Honeydew Mansion and do what...? Oh, let me not think of that and instead be grateful to be useful right now.

But go near a crime site? No never again! A promise I'll keep to myself.

Yes, Thaddeus, I'm here foremost, to see if I can find out more about Miss Platt's routines and behaviours. I'm sitting ready as a primed cannon. It's about time my cousin Finley gets closure on who his mother is–if ever there is closure to this case–and Thaddeus can rest assured I helped his sister.

With one ear, I'm listening for Gertie's trampling feet as she's about to go out and collect my mail from Miss Hermine Tow at the post office. These walls are paper thin and the girl clomps like an elephant. When I hear the front door close, I unlock my secretaire to give Thaddeus's clippings another examination.

I KNOW I'll have a good hour before Gertie returns, as that's about the time these two gossiping young women take to pass back and forth all their latest titbits of news. Mind you, Hermine Tow is a few years older than my Gertie and a bit of a peacock, but I assume they've known each other since being at Saint Mary's Primary.

The menfolk are particularly taken in by Miss Tow's good looks and charm. Butcher Wilson makes quite a fuss of his courtship for her, as does Vicar Middlemiss, but I don't think Hermine is interested in either of them.

She's only interested in herself and in what passes through her fingers.

Oh, I can see that Miss Tow's as pretty as she's sharp, but I trust her as little as the fly on my pudding. I wouldn't be surprised the creature holds specific personal envelopes over a pan of steaming water to read their contents.

Not my letters–she won't think those interesting, though she could be very wrong there–but of young lovers writing to each other. On those kinds of letters, the postmistress absolutely has her eye. Probably reads them to Gertie in her back room. Why else would she put up the closed sign every time my maid heads over there? Ah well, it's none of my business. Not what's on my plate.

With Jasper's belly full and Miss Platt hidden in her dark shop, let me see if I can find another clue. There are five clippings from *The Cotswold Times* from between 1840 and the beginning of 1846 that need my special attention.

I'm quite convinced that it's on those articles that Thaddeus based his theory: that Miss Platt is Sir Finley Lowther's biological mother. I told you that, didn't I, that that was Thaddeus's theory? Dear Lord, I'm as forgetful as a goldfish.

But anyway, that's what my benedict thought, though he didn't share it with our brother-in-law as Thaddeus wasn't given the time to prove anything definitively. He did share with me the evidence he'd gathered and I told him it seemed a wild theory, but reading these clippings, it could be plausible. Yet still wild.

∾

THADDEUS ALSO TOLD me he got the clippings from young Theresa Philpot, who succeeded her father as a reporter at *The Cotswold Times*. I think it's rather unheard of for a woman to be a reporter, but what do I know? I never met her. She could be nice and docile as like as not.

LET'S start with this first clipping of October 1845 when Addison Philpot, Miss Philpot's father, wrote:

The Cotswold Times

Wench Gone Missing from Dartmond

by Addison Philpot

Tuesday 7 October 1845

Miss Eloise Platt, daughter of Mr Nat Platt and Mrs Flossie Platt and sister to Beatrice Platt-Jones, was missing from Dartmond since Friday.

In the morning of 3 October, the 16-year-old wench left her parents' haberdasher shop on Darren Street in Dartmond to deliver a parcel at Gladmers Manor but never arrived. No trace was found of her since.

A large search party led by Constable Mortimer Walsh, with help from the Landdulton constabulary, is combing Tiversack Lake and Hungry Summit Hills. The October storms are hindering the operation.

Dartmond once again fears an attack from the unknown Hungry Summit Hills' murderer, also called 'the vagrant', though this time the villain seems to have struck in the autumn.

Since 1840, three other wenches disappeared and were found dead under mysterious circumstances. We remember Fannie Fitget in April 1840, Constance Griffin in May 1842, and Manda Turner in April last year.

Hence, we all fear for Miss Eloise Platt's fate.

~

IN HIS SPIDERY hand that I sometimes find hard to decipher, my benedict has noted:

–Note the October disappearance instead of springtime.

Miss Philpot specifically told me her father had noted this as an anomaly as well and had discussed it with Constable Mortimer Walsh, father of the current Constable Columbus Walsh (who used to be my assistant, now Dartmond's constable, but an absolute useless washcloth). There are no recordings of Mortimer Walsh left on these cases.

Columbus Walsh certainly hasn't discovered America despite his first name. He's as slow as can be. Asked him several times about his father's 1840s investigations into these murders, but he just shrugs and repeats his father never told him anything and he didn't ask. Useful information gone down the drain. All we have are these newspaper clippings.

Must say, though, that Theresa Philpot was highly interested in this regional history. Kept asking me to become involved. Didn't disclose to her this was a delicate family matter. Just warded her off. Not an unfriendly woman, but a tad too militant. Wants to take over police work if she gets a chance.

Her questions made me look more closely into the earlier murders. Sad cases indeed. Apparently abused and strangled with a cord and left on the spot of the crime. After 1845 (or 1844, if Eloise Platt didn't fall victim to the vagrant) there were no more recorded vanishings of girls. Either the murderer went elsewhere, or he died in some manner.

I'VE READ this article five times now and I can't find anything new that Thaddeus hasn't mentioned. I only make a note I'll visit that libertine reporter of *The Cotswold Times* myself to see if I can find out something fresh from her.

Let me just quickly skip to the window to see if the coast is still clear regarding Gertie. Yes, post office sign still reads 'closed, will be back soon'. It's a good thing my eyesight is so strong because that red façade of Miss Hermine's small abode is quite far to my left.

"Ah, my Jasper... No, go back to sleep, my darling." He raised his head as I went past him, the dear one.

Now, let's check out clipping number two and see if I've missed anything in that one.

The Cotswold Times

Four Dead in Coach Accident Near Tiversack

by Addison Philpot

Thursday 9 October 1845

A serious coach accident yesterday on the Lockedows Road between Tiversack and Bristol has left four people dead.

Coach driver John Cadden from Dartmond is one victim. Farmer Miller Martin, his pregnant wife Lottie, and their two-year-old daughter Margaret, from Dartmond parish, also have found their untimely deaths.

In a statement Constable Mortimer Walsh clarified it is most likely that uprooted trees due to this week's heavy storms caused the accident. The coach will have gotten off-track and landed upside-down fifty feet below in Lockedows Ravine.

The operation to hoist up the coach to see if it had other defects is still underway.

Walsh also shared that a grey shawl belonging to the missing Eloise Platt was found nearby in Lockedows Ravine. The wench has been missing for a week now.

More news on the wake for Mr John Cadden and the Martin family in Trinity Church, Dartmond, will be in tomorrow's newspaper.

~

THADDEUS ADDED:

–Awful accident but can't stop thinking what Eloise Platt's shawl was doing there in Lockedows Ravine. Pity we can't retrace whether Constable Walsh Sr. combed the site for other signs of a crime except for the accident.

What if Eloise Platt was also on that coach and survived? But that's just wild imagination. Got nothing to stake it on. The coach was heading for Bristol. Why would a Dartmond underaged girl want to go to Bristol when she's probably not been further than Landdulton all her life? No, it's more likely she lost that shawl when she was grabbed by that murdering vagrant. But then again, she wasn't murdered as the latter clipping shows. She went missing for three months. Three months, late in the year! Where can she have been? Did that culprit hide her somewhere?

~

MY DEAR THADDEUS is clearly racking his brain over our Miss Platt here. I remember that time so well when he couldn't let it go. He was so ill already, terrible stomach aches, and I just wanted him to lie on his bed, but he wouldn't listen. He was obsessed with the case, so much so that although I also wanted it solved for my cousin and Thaddeus's sister's sake, I began to hate Eloise Platt and the whole assumption she had something to do with Finley's adoption.

Let me look at the next clipping.

The Cotswolds Times

Dangerous Villain Suspected of Another Spring Murder

by Addison Philpot

Wednesday 17 April 1845

The unknown murderer in Hungry Summit Hills has most likely struck again. This time victim is fifteen-year-old Manda Turner, daughter of cobbler Tommy Turner and his late wife Eugenie, of 12 Darren Street, Dartmond. The unfortunate wench was found dead at the foot of Lockedows Hill on Tuesday.

Details of her death–presumed murder–have not been disclosed by Constable Mortimer Walsh. However, Walsh urges parents to be more vigilant regarding their young daughters.

We remember the sad cases of Fannie Fitget in 1840 and Constance Griffin in 1842. All traces lead to the unknown vagrant who apparently roams Hungry Summit Hills but has never been identified. The wenches' deaths show gruesome similarities, according to Walsh, and early spring seems this predator's season.

The wake for Manda Turner will be held in Trinity Church, Dartmond, on Thursday 18 April at 7.00 p.m.

THADDEUS ADDED:

—These murders are certainly the work of the same man, but Eloise Platt's going missing in October doesn't fit the pattern. I'm just glad this awful business stopped in 1845. Must have wrecked a close-knit community like Dartmond.

I'm tired. It's that Finley says his father told him he was adopted at birth, but could the old squire have been delirious? His wife was sent to an asylum shortly after Eloise Platt returned to Dartmond, so it could all just be a coincidence.

Maybe we're all on the wrong trail and only Eloise Platt can tell us where she was those three months she went missing. If she doesn't start talking soon, she'll probably take the secret with her into the grave. As far as I know, nobody has ever forced her to talk because she was so traumatized and in hospital for quite a while, according to what Theresa had gathered from her father. If she went to Landdulton Hospital, the doctors must have known whether she'd ever been with child, but that is always confidential information no hospital will share.

~

Oh, my poor, poor husband. Of course, he was exhausted. It's such a rigmarole. I know Finley did everything to help Thaddeus with the investigation, but he wasn't very keen on the idea someone as lowly as Eloise Platt could have borne him. And I can't blame him. Finley is a fine man with an excellent education and a lovely wife, my sister-in-law.

Anna and Thaddeus are so similar in their good-natured kindness. I quite miss the Lowthers' company now I've moved away and don't have the living quarters to entertain. And I've not had the heart to travel much by coach and visit them at Gladmers Manor.

HERE'S another tidbit of information for you. I've known the Lowthers all my life–they are my family in more than one way. Catherine and Finley are my cousins, as my mother was a Lowther, Sir Reginald's sister. And Thaddeus's sister Anna married my cousin Finley. Now you get the full picture of why it is so important that I solve this, it is fully a family matter, not just a promise to Thaddeus.

Finley is Gladmers's next squire, of course, but when Sir Reginald turned his son's entire life upside down just before departing this earthly life, it proved detrimental to Finley's health. He's always had heart problems, but they seem to have gotten worse with this unverified adoption. It's not like Sir Reginald showed Finley any papers proving the adoption.

We just don't know what Sir Reginald's will means. Just that Finley has to try to find his biological mother and pay her money, on Sir Reginald's request.

Anyway, Gladmers Manor has always been one of my favourite places in the world because it's where I met my dear benedict. But that's a story for another time. Let's go back to these wretched newspaper clippings. Two more left in Thaddeus' file with notes: Lady Kittie's hospitalization and Eloise's return.

The Cotswolds Times

Lady Kittie Admitted to Ridgeview Asylum

by Addison Philpot

Thursday 18 January 1846

According to Doctor Jennings Alardice of Ridgeview Asylum, Squire Reginald Lowther's spouse, Lady Kittie Lowther, has been hospitalised at Ridgeview Asylum for an indefinite time.

No information was shared on Lady Lowther's health, except that she gave birth to a son, Finley Reginald Lowther, on Christmas Day, and has been unwell since.

Also, after the birth of their three-year-old daughter Catherine, Lady Lowther suffered from post-natal symptoms and has since seldom shown herself in society since.

The people of Dartmond and Landdulton rejoice in the birth of the Squire's son, who is the heir to the Gladmers estate. Despite the sorrow of her illness, Lady Kittie's unexpected Christmas baby was a present to all.

An evocation for Lady Kittie Lowther's health will be held at Trinity Church, Dartmond, on Saturday 20 January at 7.00 p.m.

∽

THADDEUS'S NOTES READ:

–Another sad event. I knew Lady Kittie as a little boy when we went over to Gladmers Manor, where my father was the Squire's gamekeeper. I even vaguely remember Sir Reginald and Miss Kittie's wedding, as it was such a grand affair. All of Dartmond and Landdulton had seen "nothing as posh as that since Queen Victoria's wedding to Prince Albert". My mother's words, not mine.

And the most beautiful outcome of my father's work was, of course, later meeting my wife-to-be at Gladmers. Miss Imogene Bowditch. She was the talk of the town. Such prettiness and accomplishment from London. How could I ever have dreamt she would marry a lowly man like myself? But she did!

That's why this is such a sad message. Lady Kittie was frail, truth be told, but it's so long ago, no one remembers her.

Those first years after our marriage, we would spend so many delightful occasions together at Gladmers with Finley and Anna, picnics and soirees. We even did a boat trip down to Oxford. Just the four of us. Anna, Finley, Imogene and I. And Finley was my best man at our wedding. Ah, such sadness. It makes my heart bitter.

∿

I MUST PAUSE HERE for a moment as Thaddeus's words bring tears to my eyes. I didn't know he'd mixed his investigation with personal notes. I had read the clippings, but I'd refrained from going over my benedict's notes, as I knew they would tear at my heart. All these wonderful memories when we were young and unburdened by the toils and tribulations of adult life.

∿

WHERE'S THAT AWFUL MAID? I think I need some lunch, after all. Mind you, I'm not hungry; my stomach is queasy and my heart heavy. A sure sign I need something solid inside.

You know what? I'll take a brief break before I read the last clipping on Eloise's return. I'll go to the kitchen to prepare myself a sandwich. That will awake old Jasper, and I could do with a bit of his company.

"Come on, dearie, let's have some lunch, shall we?" He can be quick if he wants and toddles behind me like a baby duck after its mother. We're just two old souls, he and I, but we'll manage. Even without the staff.

I take the wrapped egg and bacon sandwich Gertie, with some sense of thoughtfulness, has left for me on the counter. Jasper gobbles up his half faster than I do. I sit at my kitchen table, a rare occasion for me, as this place is so strange and different from my light and spacious kitchen in Honeydew Mansion and the cheerful chatter of Mrs Peaton. The bread tastes dry in my mouth, but it does its work in my stomach. Wash it down with the last of the tea and hope for the best.

Doctor Ed Rule, my wonderful doctor and friend in Landdulton, who helped me so much with all my feminine ailments–bless his soul–told me this simple trick. The old fox knew, of course, that I skip meals when no one's paying attention.

"Get something inside you, Imogene, and you'll feel in fine fettle within seconds. Food is the antidote to a quivering mind in your case."

He is so right, the dear doctor. Oh, another soul I miss. I'm not looking forward to being treated by Edmund Suthmeer, should I need him at my bedside.

That doctor doesn't seem to have half the wits Dr Rule had. Dr Suthmeer is that old-fashioned type of doctor with his high, stiff white collars, black-velvet knicker-bockers, and plumed hat. And then that eternal frown as if his patients wear him more down every day.

Can't people just move a little with the times, espe-cially in professions where they tend to the needs of others? Who wants such an antique-looking doctor sticking his nose in your bedchambers?

But I'm being side-tracked by my own thoughts.

"Let's go back in and grasp the nettle again, Jasper dear. The mistress must come up with a plan before 1895 rolls to an end. With all my sad reminiscing over my good life in Landdulton. I might change my mind and move back there in spite of Miss Platt's shop in Dartmond. I don't fit in here at all and all my watching for six months hasn't achieved much of anything."

All right, last clipping. Miss Platt miraculously reap-pears in Dartmond. Let's see what Thaddeus remarked on this.

~

The Cotswolds Times

A Christmas Miracle: Eloise Platt Has Returned Home

by Addison Philpot

Boxing Day 26 December 1845

Sixteen-year-old Eloise Platt has safely returned to her

parents' house on Darren Street, Dartmond. "This is a Christmas Miracle," her father Nat Platt announced. The family has asked for some privacy as Eloise is badly shaken and unable to talk of her ordeals yet.

Constable Mortimer Walsh hopes that Miss Platt's survival will provide a proper description of the unknown vagrant who took the lives of Fannie Fitget, Constance Griffin, and Manda Turner.

However, it is uncertain if Eloise Platt's disappearance is related to the above cases, and if so, how she was able to escape.

A Gratitude Mass for Eloise Platt's safe return to Dartmond society will be held on Saturday 27 December in Trinity Church, Dartmond at 7.00 p.m.

THADDEUS NOTES ARE:

—This article, together with Finley's account of his father's revelation about his adoption, is what made some pieces of the puzzle fall into place. In my opinion, Eloise can't have fallen prey to the same vagrant who killed the other girls, or she wouldn't have returned.

Most likely—if she was at all pregnant—it was by someone from Dartmond. Alas, fifty years later it will be hard to find out who that was, unless it comes from her own mouth. I've tried in my function as the Cotswolds' chief constable to ask her for an interview, but as there were no charges against her and her name was mentioned nowhere in relation to

Gladmers Manor, Miss Platt rightfully refused to talk with me.

And then there was that weasel Columbus Walsh telling me to mind my own shop and let him rule over Dartmond. I should have fired him then, but as an honour to his father, who was a top policeman, and because it's so hard to find reliable officers in this region, I bit my tongue and swallowed my loss. Miss Platt will not talk, under any circumstances, which—as any self-respecting policeman knows—speaks of a guilty mind.

My dear Imogene, I trust that you, with your feminine touch and better manners, will get her to talk at some point. I lay all my faith in your beautiful hands. Now you prove my theory, dear.

THADDEUS's last words almost run off the page and are hardly readable. Oh, how ill he was at the time! Lying in his bed in front of the window overlooking Tiversack Lake, so thin and pale. Unable to eat anything of substance. Just a little soup and lukewarm tea. Oh, oh, oh, my dear old heart is in so much pain right now.

He wrote this only a few days before he passed. Still remember his glasses slipping down his nose and his hand with the pen shaking so much he was almost crying from the effort. Can you imagine, a grown man crying because he can't solve a case and can't write what he needs to write? It would break the devil's heart if he had one.

Let me not go there, please, dear Lord. That awful 17th of April. A cold, dreary Wednesday morning. Oh, I shudder when my mind takes me back there. I forbid myself that today. I've got work to do.

Like giving my final thoughts on Miss Platt's return to Dartmond and the fact she survived another fifty years with her secret only known to herself. I have another fear, though. I didn't know Thaddeus had tried to get Miss Platt to talk. She will suspect my arrival here opposite her shop. But what can I do? How I wish I had not avoided Thaddeus's notes for so many months!

I need to go outside and buy myself that new red folder. It's so stuffy in this room and the coal fire smells dreadful. I might even go for a short walk and see if Janie Lewis has finally received those latest London patterns.

Ah, sometimes I can't stand this backwater, though Janie's a good dressmaker.

Bah, Imogene, don't look down on life here. The Cotswolds have given you the happiest years of your life!

Let me first check if it has stopped snowing, or I won't be able to go out at all. Yes, and the Fritters' boys are clearing the snow from the pavements. That's a pair of helpful lads. Ah, and there's Gertie crossing the street with my mail, so let me jot my notes under this last clipping.

I'll follow where you've led me, Thaddeus. I'll visit Glad-mers Manor and talk everything over once more with Finley and Anna. I'll also contact Theresa Philpot and ask her to repeat what she told you. I might even try my hand at Columbus Walsh and, of course, I'll find a reason to interview Miss Platt.

"Come on, Jasper, wake up and comfort the missus. She's as sad as angels for a good man's sin."

4

A VISIT TO GLADMERS MANOR AND A STRANGE TURN OF EVENTS

Gladmers Manor, 1 January 1896

I will not waste too many words on my Christmas celebrations this year. It was sober; it was solitary; and it was self-absorbed. In the end, I declined the Boxing Day invitation to the Pococks, after all. Just wasn't up to it.

I'll do better in 1896. I promise. I've got my plan ready for action, and today I've ordered the coach to take me to Gladmers Manor.

Now I've bitten the bullet to socialize again, I'm actually looking forward to seeing Finley and Anna. It's been way too long. Last saw them on that sad, sad day of Thaddeus's funeral.

Nicest, warmest day of all April, and so much bitterness in the air mingling with the sweet fruity scent of the wisteria vines in Grand Lake Cemetery. I can't look back on that day without getting a heart full of sorrow.

I'll tell coach driver Cadden to pass by the cemetery

to ask my Thaddeus for some guidance. My little head-to-head with Miss Platt just before Christmas and the study of the clippings has left me hemming and hawing on how to proceed with the case. So, I need some help from above.

Oh, my dear Jasper is on pins and needles. He knows so well when I'm going out without him, but I really can't take him with me today. No matter, I keep telling him I'll be back before five; he is as restless as the desert wind. Getting up and lying on top of my feet, then back on his throne and then yapping at the door.

I haven't left him here on his own in Dartmond but he's going to get extra sausage from Gertie, and I've told Neil Fritter to take him for a walk in the afternoon. Mind you, that's my next worry because I'm leaving Gertie unchaperoned with that fine fishmonger's lad, who's got arms like a boat worker and a good mop of strawberry-blond hair to top his neat face. Ah well, I can't control everything.

It's a calm first day of January, with a soft chilly breeze rising from Tiversack Lake, but there's also a promising winter sun up in the sky. As I stare out of my coach window, a tangle of thoughts and feelings consume me.

I've taken Lakeside Path so often with my benedict, in all seasons. This road between Landdulton and Dartmond was always one of our favourites. On the one side you have the glistening water of Tiversack Lake and on the other side, the sloping climb of Hungry Summit Hills, now decked with snow. The pine trees are raising their powdered tops to the sky, and the only traces in the snow are the footprints of hares and deer.

Wild nature has never been very alluring to me, as I

grew up in the hustle and bustle of central London. My daily sights were horse-drawn carts and carriages passing by. Nature rides meant going to Hyde Park on Sunday in Papa's Landauer. In the summers we might go to Brighton for a walk on the seaside. The visits to the Cotswolds with my mother, were the extent of my nature development.

Thaddeus was an out-of-doors man through-and-through. He did his best to teach me the delights of the West Country and succeeded to some extent, as he was such a passionate teacher. So, it's due to him I can now appreciate this winter day with my hot-water bottle at my feet and a warm rug around my knees. The swaying of the carriage has a lulling effect on my overtaxed brain.

I forgot to tell you; I never got the red folder from Hopewell's. After the strange visit to Miss Platt's shop, I was quite done with being outside and went straight to Donald's to get his permission to let Neil carry Jasper up and down the stairs. Then I went home and closed the curtains, as I was suffering from one of my rare migraines.

Thaddeus's brown, coffee-stained file is here by my side. My family visit will be a social event as much as discussing this Christmas baby thing with Finley and Anna. It may be a repetition of the talk Thaddeus and I had with them last year, but I hope I'll get some fresh perspective.

When the carriage bounces into the winding driveway to Gladmers Manor, I'm struck as always how secluded the estate is from the rest of the world. As if one's eyes are closed to reality when entering the Lowthers' property.

From three sides, the full-grown forest keeps the

manor out of sight. Only the back of the house, facing Tiversack Lake, has a sloping lawn towards the shoreline.

The branches of the oak trees on either side of the driveway almost touch each other so that they regularly hit the coach, and Jack Cadden's curses on his box that he can hardly pass through.

It's true, Sir Reginald Lowther, my mother's brother, and their father Finley Sr. both had a firm streak of the eccentric. Mind you, I liked my grandfather and my uncle. Especially my Uncle Reginald. He always had these wild ideas during our summer visits.

Being an amateur-engineer, he had built a kind of motorized boat–it looked more like a bathtub with rotor blades behind it–and he wanted to take me along for a ride in it on Tiversack Lake. Mother was horrified her brother would suggest such a thing to her young daughter, but I was ecstatic. Scooped up my petticoats and stepped right into the boat. It didn't start though, and that was the end of it.

My cousin Catherine, Uncle Reginald and Aunt Kittie's only daughter, inherited that wild touch from her father. Latest I heard, she was studying the pyramids in Egypt.

Anyway, my mind is meandering again. It makes sense that Finley wouldn't be their son. If there was one straitlaced Victorian gentleman, it would be Finley Lowther. Never seen much emotion in him, not even when he came to tell us about the shocking news he was adopted.

Ah well, he said in that slightly pedantic voice of his, *I just hope my biological parents were honest and god-fearing folk.*

From the moment his father told him about his adoption, he showed ambivalence about tracking them down. I think he's afraid of who they might be, even though he's secure and safe as Gladmers squire.

"Thad is so good at unravelling these things. Maybe your parents are from the region and still alive. It's worth trying to find them, Fin. Maybe you'll even turn out to have more brothers and sisters. And it was your father's dying wish."

He'd shrugged. "Maybe my father made a misstep. Anyway, I have Catherine and that's more than I can handle for a sibling."

In that, my cousin is right. As the squire and heir to the estate, he must govern his sister's affairs.

I'm not sure, but I think I told you it was at Catherine's wedding that I met Thaddeus? Well, Catherine has since been estranged from her husband. Half the time we don't even know where she is until we get a postcard from China, or South America, and now two months ago from Egypt. Could Finley's parentage affect Catherine's inheritance as well? We do not know the details of the will, but I pray to God it won't.

Ah, there's a glimpse of the grand house through the snow-laden trees. The peaks of the rooftops are covered in snow.

Coachman Cadden is whoa-whoaing the horses to a slow trot. Suddenly, I'm nervous. What if something terrible happened here fifty years ago that sent my Aunt Kittie over the edge? I've never had these shivers before when I visited Gladmers Manor, but with what I've read in the clippings, it's all becoming a jumble in my head. I hope I'm not getting another migraine.

The fresh air does me good as I descend from the coach with Cadden's help. He's not said one word to me, but I'm used to that. He means well; he's just a bit grim.

"Come and collect me at two, Cadden. I want to be back in Dartmond before dark."

I've already told him I want to pass by Grand Lake Cemetery on the way back. He just taps his cap and hops back on the box. He's quite an agile man at his age, though one wonders exactly what age. Nondescript person altogether.

As the coach turns round and the horses' hooves clippity-clop back along the driveway, I stand looking up at the big house with the file under my arm and my hands tucked into my rabbit fur muff.

Red brick walls, steeply pitched roofs, ornate gables, painted iron railings, canted bay windows. Early Victorian architecture. My grandfather, the first Finley Lowther, built it in 1830 after the old house burnt down. Don't know the details of the fire, and I'm more interested in the current house.

It is as if I'm seeing Gladmers Manor for the first time. Really seeing it. It's a peculiar house that hides a mystery. I'm sensitive to these things, although Thaddeus would call that hocus pocus.

Something happened here that hasn't seen the light of day. But what? I trudge up the three stone steps to the ornate front door and let the knocker with the lion's head come down twice. Then I take a deep breath.

A young maid in a black dress and white apron opens the door.

"Are Lord and Lady Lowther back from Church?"

In her thick accent she answers, "Yes, Mrs Lynch, they're expecting you in the parluh. Do come in."

"All right, thank you."

I follow her through the long corridor to the back of the house that overlooks the meadows with deer and glittering Tiversack Lake in the distance. The house smells of passed-their-bloom lilies, which is rather pungent and unpleasant.

I hand my coat and muff to the maid and, armed only with the file, step into Finley and Anna's parlour.

They both rise from their chairs near the hearth when I come in. It strikes me again how tall Anna is, the same height as her husband, her sweet face so like that of Thaddeus. Generous, clear blue-grey eyes with dark lashes, the same smile.

Finley has grown even stouter, the buttons of his pinstriped waistcoat can no longer close, and his cheeks are red-veined and full. He seems even more morose, unhappy with himself. They both come towards me, and we shake hands. We've never been too affectionate with each other. There is no necessity for ostentatious gestures when one has a good rapport with one's family.

"Imogene, you look well. We were so pleased with your letter telling us you would finally come." Anna points to the extra chair at the hearth and we sit.

"I'm glad to be out of the house. I apologize for not inviting you to Dartmond yet. I haven't been entertaining so far. Oh, it's good to be with you at Gladmers after all this time." I hear myself say and my voice thankfully sounds cheerful.

Anna does most of the talking as usual, while Finley smokes his cigar and looks from one of us to the other.

"We perfectly understand that, Imogene. And we didn't want to press ourselves upon you but we have been wondering how you were faring in that strange new town. You write the apartment isn't very grand. Nothing like Honeydew Mansion, that you so dote on?"

There's hesitation in her voice. *Am I saying the right thing?* Sympathy creases her face, and the lines show the loss of her beloved brother.

"It's basic. I can't say otherwise, and I won't stay there for longer than absolutely necessary. Nine months have been way too long already, but it has its use for now." I'm aware of sounding a little cryptic, but don't want to turn the topic to my reasons for my cramped housing so soon after arriving at my hosts' place.

"Would you care for a small sherry, Imogene?" Finley's eyes are already darting longingly to the decanter as he asks it.

In a moment of boldness, I utter, "Why not? I'm usually not one for alcoholic drinks, but it is a festive occasion to be reunited with you."

"Exactly." My cousin is already heaving his ample build from the armchair to busy himself with the crystal decanter and glasses.

"I've told Mrs White to have lunch ready at noon. I hope that suits you?" Anna chimes in. I nod, not looking forward to having my tiny mouse bites exposed in public. I know Anna is aware that my appetite has suffered from losing Thaddeus, but I warn her, nonetheless.

"You haven't ordered your housekeeper to prepare an extravagant lunch? You know I have the appetite of a hummingbird."

"Do not worry." Anna smiles Thaddeus's smile, which

both warms and breaks my heart all over again. "Just some light oxtail soup and yesterday's shepherd's pie. Nothing fancy. Fin and I don't eat large lunches either. We prefer a large tea and an appropriate supper." I know this not to be the truth, but I appreciate her diplomacy.

We all raise our glasses to toast to the new year. What is 1896 going to bring us? Closure or not? I feel the apprehension and the anticipation in all three of us.

The scent of the sherry - sweet sultanas and raisins with a hint of liquorice - drifts into my nose before I take a sip. I'm instantly transported back to Tiversack Inn where we went after we'd buried my benedict. That smell, the agony, the view over the water in bright spring sunshine. A moment frozen in time. My life adrift.

I swallow hard before taking a sip, forcing myself to stay anchored in this room at Gladmers with my family, not broken and desolate on that first day without my life companion.

The sherry is sweet and creamy but still burns in my throat. I feel Anna's clever eyes resting on me.

"Just leave it if it doesn't suit you. I can ring the bell for a glass of elderflower lemonade. You still don't drink coffee?"

I shake my head. "It's all right, Anna, there will be more firsts after this. Let me get used to it."

Finley has already finished the contents of his glass and his hand reaches for the decanter with the amber-coloured liquor. The sherry smell seems to permeate the room, but I know it's just me with my sensitive nose. Anna's eyes follow her husbands' quick movements with an unreadable look in them.

"Brings me to another topic." Finley's voice is serious

as his eyes turn from his glass to me. "Anna and I didn't know if we had to write to you about Theresa Philpot, but we've been getting so much attention from her lately. The woman seems adamant to get her spinster nose in our affairs." Finley sounds bitter, as he sometimes does. I prick up my ears. Theresa Philpot is high on my list of persons with whom I seek an encounter.

"The long and the short of it is," Anna fills in for her husband, "we've also invited her to lunch today, as we don't know when there will be another opportunity. She says she has things she wants to share with us...you know... about that adoption affair. Mind you, we told her we hadn't discussed it with you and that you might feel outsiders as an intrusion on our family lunch. Theresa said it would be no problem to return home if you objected to the idea." Anna's blue-grey eyes look at me helplessly. Finley hides behind his sherry glass.

I swallow one more time. This is actually more than I had hoped for. I feel as if Thaddeus has sent me on this mission. What better use of time than to get ahead with the case? Maybe my grief has turned me into a clumsy person in society, something I've never been. It is like I can't do chitchat anymore, not even with my next of kin. I want closure and normality.

"Great idea." I hope my voice is enthusiastic enough as I still struggle with the sherry. "It must have been foresight that I brought Thaddeus's file with me." I tap the brown cover next to me in the chair.

"Yes, I observed you hanging on to that folder." Finley hesitates, his thumb and forefinger pull his short salt-and-pepper beard, a gesture showing he is wrangling with something internally.

"Listen, Imogene, Anna and I talked about this before you came. We know Thaddeus wanted you to find out who my biological mother is–if it isn't Lady Lowther herself. We also know you're grappling with this and we… we want to tell you that, for our part, you are not bound by this promise." He stops, looks at his wife for help. Anna smoothly takes over.

"True, dear Imogene. Sometimes we feel it's much better to let sleeping dogs lie. We have a good life. Finley isn't in need of a mother figure or anything like that. We… sometimes believe it was more the policeman in Thaddeus who wanted to get this case revealed than that there was an urgent need for knowing who Finley is, if he isn't a Lowther by birth. We'll pay the money to the hospital and forget all about it."

I listen intently. There's a double standard here. On the one hand they invite Miss Philpot for lunch, and now they're telling me they're having second thoughts. I feel drawn to that second idea myself. Can't count the times I've regretted my promise to Thaddeus.

"I know it's upsetting the family," I hear myself say, "something that happened fifty years ago and seems none of our business anymore. But… I can't just ignore Thaddeus's last wish, now, can I?" Anna interrupts me.

"You can, Imogene, if you see the entire case as the wish of the policeman detective who felt it is his duty to dig up the truth. But think a little more. Would Thaddeus have wanted us to be all miserable with this information gathering once he'd realised the people involved weren't keen on finding out the truth?"

"But why did you invite Miss Philpot then?"

Finley gestures to Anna, who shrugs.

"Because we think you'll be the only one who can tell her to stop digging. Drop the entire case. We've already tried to convince her, but to no avail. There's really nothing she can add to what you have in that file. Her father passed away in 1850, when she was only three years old. She knows nothing more than we know. She says that from a reporter's standpoint, this is 'such an interesting case'. Can you imagine? Calling poor Finley 'an interesting case'? My hairs rise on my arms when I hear her talk like that. So, please Imogene, just convince Miss Philpot to stop bothering us." Anna looks at me with doe eyes and I feel myself nodding.

"I agree. I wish there was a nice way out for all of us. If Miss Platt won't talk, it will never be solved. Unless she has nothing to do with it," I contradict myself.

"We have nothing to gain and either ay ten per cent of the inheritance is paid out. With that done, Miss Philpot can just shut upup," Finley summarises when there's a knock on the door and Mrs White announces lunch and the arrival of Miss Philpot.

With my head in a spin, I follow my hosts to the luxurious dining room in the west wing of Gladmers. *Oh Thaddeus, what am I to do?* I really don't know anymore.

A tiny woman in a simple brown dress with white cuffs and sleeves stands with her back to us, warming her hands at the fire. When she turns, I'm pleasantly surprised to see an attractive, middle-aged woman with fine features and lively, violet eyes, beautiful auburn hair done up in a stylish bun. Quite a lady and equally self-assured. Her own woman, the kind I like. Sometimes. A ready smile curls Miss Philpot's lips as Anna introduces us.

"I've heard so much about you, Mrs Lynch! What a wonderful treat to finally meet you, but do tell if I'm interrupting a family lunch."

"Not at all." I smile back. "It's nice to make your acquaintance. I gather you met with my late husband quite a few times?"

"Oh yes, I did. I always say the first to arrive at the site of a crime are the police and the reporter. In a way our jobs are very similar, but we go about it in a different way. But please forgive my bad manners. My sincere condolences, Mrs Lynch. Your husband was such a fine man and a great policeman. He's greatly missed in Landdulton society."

I accept her condolences reverently.

"Please, let's have lunch." That is Finley, who's eying the soup getting cold on the porcelain plates. The four of us sit at a corner of the long dinner table that can seat at least twenty people. I remember this table so well. Most of our summer holidays were spent here with Mama and sometimes Papa when he wasn't abroad with his army regiment. Also, every other Christmas, the years we didn't celebrate it with the Bowditches in London.

As soon as the meal starts, Finley only has eyes for the food and doesn't take part much in the conversation. I find myself in an animated discourse with Miss Philpot and Anna on the differences between Landdulton and Dartmond. Miss Philpot has lived in both.

"I always say Landdulton is more bourgeoise and Dartmond more working class. And what do you think I prefer?" The ready smile is back on her face.

"I honestly wouldn't know," I reply. "I haven't decided

myself which town I prefer. They are so unalike. So, pray tell me your thoughts, Miss Philpot."

The violet eyes dart around the table but only catch mine. Anna is watching her husband ordering the footman to serve him a second helping of the shepherd's pie. My first small portion is still lying crumbled in the middle of an enormous white plate decorated with painted ivy leaves.

"Dartmond, of course!" Miss Philpot seems elated about her preference, which I find intriguing but can't follow.

"Please enlighten me. Now I've set up camp there, I might as well be informed about its charms."

"Oh, but dear Mrs Lynch, I do think you see it with those sharp eyes of yours!" Miss Philpot has come totally alive in this town comparison, and I wonder if it's the effect of the sherry, or that she's generally so full of vim and vigour. I quite like it. It's a bit of a stir in my solemn life.

"As I'm right front and centre in Darren Street, I can see that Dartmond is more colloquial and easier going than Landdulton. Dartmonders seem more themselves and not so worried about what the rest of the town will say about them behind their backs," I contemplate aloud, not really understanding where these observations come from.

"Fie, Imogene! I'd never have expected *you* to like Dartmond of all places. You, who were raised among the finest of the fine in London's Kensington." Anna is clearly shocked, and I check my tongue.

For some reason, the discussion in Miss Platt's shop about Dartmond possibly getting a half-Indian mayor flits back into my mind. The sherry surely has gone to *my* head. I'm not a radical, am I? Heavens, Thaddeus's firm, guiding hand is very much missed here.

A little sterner than before, I look at Miss Philpot. Could she be one of these libertine women? The last time I read *The Illustrated London News*, there was this article about women overseas in America taking all sorts of liberties. Declaring they want to have the right to divorce their husbands, even to be entitled to vote. I have heard no mention of a Mr Philpot. Is she one of these free-thinkers, and should I steer clear of her?

I decide to change the subject. Just to be on the safe side.

"Well, anyway, I'm in Dartmond for a reason, which is also the reason we're here together. I understand from my cousin that you are intrigued by this secret Christmas baby mystery, Miss Philpot?" I feel all eyes on me and my cheeks colour. I may have missed the mark again. I've lost all sense of etiquette and am surely going about it in the wrong way.

It's silent for a while and I'm aware Miss Philpot is studying Anna and Finley instead of addressing my question. Then she says with a nervous tremor in her voice but shiny, excited eyes.

"Yes, very. I couldn't wait to meet with you, Mrs Lynch. I'm afraid I have no new information for you yet, but I intend to travel to Bristol next week where they have more extensive newspaper archives than here in Land-dulton. This is what I also offered to do for your late husband, but we... we ran out of time." Finley audibly clears his throat and I sense Anna's eyes on me, so I interrupt Miss Philpot's flow of words.

"That won't be necessary, Miss Philpot, as we..."

Unperturbed, the reporter continues, as if she hasn't even heard my words and I'm temporarily too baffled to interrupt her again. The audacity of the woman. My cheeks colour again.

"There's not just what my father reported in *The Cotswolds Times*, you know the clippings that I provided to your late husband. Perhaps we can find other articles from *The Cirencester Daily* or even in *The Bristol Times* that give us more detailed information on the strange happenings in the 1840s. Or anything that mentions a high-profile adoption. For that reason, I intend to travel to London to search the national adoption registers."

"Miss Philpot!"

My voice is sharp, too sharp as a guest at somebody else's table but there seems no stopping her otherwise. It works, she shuts up, waits, shares renewed glances with the Lowthers, and to my surprise bites her lip.

"Sorry," I mumble, "we're just not sure whether we want to go ahead with investigating Sir Finley's birth circumstances, Miss Philpot."

Finley has finished with his shepherd's pie and dabs his clean-shaven, ruby cheeks with the white damask napkin. He comes to my aid.

"There's really no need to pursue it further, Miss Philpot. Before you arrived, we discussed with Mrs Lynch that it was perhaps best to let the whole matter rest. And for me, that's..." He looks straight at me now. "... the end of it."

I'm not sure what I'm feeling, regret or relief. I understand Finley's afraid Miss Philpot will go on her search, anyway. I'm so confused that I don't know what to say.

Anna comes to the rescue as usual. She seems to see me fight with my promise to Thaddeus.

"Finley's only saying there is no hurry, Imogene. You have enough on your mind as it is. You can both let it rest for the time being, can't you?"

Miss Philpot now fixes her violet reporter eyes on me, and I see the eagerness has not subsided in them. Actually, quite similar to Thaddeus when he was on a trail. She was right when she compared reporters to detectives. They share common traits. But I'm neither.

My family here wants to protect me from getting too worried about this whole thing. And it's true it's as heavy on my stomach as this shepherd's pie. The scent makes me nauseous though it's fine mashed potato and the best minced lamb.

"I don't know." I hear myself say as the dessert is rolled in, apple crumble with fresh cream and cherry sauce. "Let me think on it, all right?"

I'm still confused and looking forward to putting my dilemma before Thaddeus when I walk out of Gladmers' front door and step into Cadden's coach. Suddenly I see Miss Philpot's auburn head at the carriage window. I lower it slightly as the wind is icy-cold. She hands me a piece of paper.

"Here are my details at *The Cotswold Times*. You may always reach out to me, should you have any questions. I'm at your service. But if you decide not to go ahead with this case, I'll do it on my own."

And she's gone. I see her hoist up her skirts, even

showing her white petticoats, and get on a bicycle. She cycles away as if she does nothing else all day. I look at the slip of paper.

The Cotswolds Times
Miss T.R. Philpot
Head Reporter
25 Hungry Summit Lane
Landdulton

I SHAKE my head in wonder. Here's as stubborn a woman as you have them. She frightens me a little. As if she is manifesting Thaddeus's request. Should I continue? But what about Finley and Anna? They want the case dropped. Finley may already have paid that hospital for all I know. Not that money is an issue here. The Lowthers are the richest family in the neighbourhood.

I tuck Miss Philpot's slip of paper in the file and try to forget her and her violet eyes. To concentrate on my task ahead.

When we arrive at Grand Lake Cemetery, it starts snowing and I order the coach driver to drive right up to Thaddeus's tombstone under the large weeping willow.

Jack opens an umbrella for me and holds it over my head as I cautiously step through the snow to my benedict's resting place. It will ruin my best shoes, but I have no choice.

"Hand me the umbrella, Jack," I say as I take it from him. I need this time on my own. Fat white snowflakes cling to my coat and whirl under the umbrella into my face. They feel like wet tears, but I know my eyes are dry.

∾

Here lies Thaddeus Walton Lynch
Born Landdulton 5 May 1839–Died Landdulton 17
April 1895
Chief Constable for The Cotswolds for 33 years
Beloved husband of Imogene Margareta Lynch-Bowditch
The winter is past. The flowers appear on the earth; the time
of the singing of birds is come.

∾

THE SPECKLED MARBLE headstone is almost covered in snow, but I can still make out Verses 2:11–12 of the Song of Solomon. Thaddeus stubbornly called it the Song of Songs. But he loved it and that's why I thought it was fitting to have it as an epitaph on his tombstone. Because he was born in spring and died just before his fifty-sixth birthday, also in spring.

As always, I first have these prosaic thoughts when I'm standing here at the foot of his grave. As if I can't mourn him here where I need to. The sadness strikes me when I'm at home in my chair or at night in my bed, but hardly ever here where his mortal body rests. His soul is with me wherever I go.

It's business, my dear, I begin. *I'm so confused with Finley's message. As if he doesn't want to know his origins and I shouldn't continue probing. But why did I move to Dartmond in the first place then? If I have nothing to seek there? Do you think he's hiding something? That he doesn't want me to continue my search? That he hates the idea of a commoner like Miss Platt possibly having given birth to him?*

And Anna, your dear sister, seems to support him in this. She was always for the truth, but I fear she's been influenced by Finley. Oh, I don't know what to do, my dear benedict. And then that nosy reporter seems to push something on me. I'm quite out of sorts and should return quickly to Jasper, as he'll be so miserable without me. But what do you say, my dear? What should I do?

I don't care one inch if the coach driver hears me mumbling. I'm really in a pickle and need to get a sign from above. I halt my verbiage and wait. Still as a church mouse, I stand while my feet become freezing cold.

Nothing. Not a twig moves. Just the silent snow falling and falling. Then the topped-up snow slides down from his headstone and lands in a heap.

Let go? Is that what's you're saying, my benedict? That I should no longer pursue Miss Platt but let it rest? Another heap tumbles down, spreading the powdered snow over Thaddeus's flat stone.

Oh, I say. Just, *oh.* Then, *Thank you.* I get one hand out of my muff and pick up a handful of the fallen snow. It's light as a feather and as purely white as a sin forgiven. I glance once more at the grave. Feel my heartbeat in my chest and then the tears come. I quickly sprinkle the snow back on the still grave, put my wet hand back in the warm muff and turn to the coach.

I've been relieved of my unwelcome duty. Then why am I so sad?

5

JUST WHEN I AM THINKING OF LETTING GO THIS HAPPENS

Dartmond, April 1896

Jasper and I survived our first winter in Dartmond. That's as much as I can say about it. I've always considered myself a person of good cheer, but I have been battling my way through these past months. So, I've had little heart-to-heart to share with you.

The only development in my investigation into whether Miss Platt is Finley's biological mother was the endless stream of letters I received from Miss Philpot. Until I was so annoyed by watching Gertie carry another lavender envelope across the street that I stopped opening them. I store them in Thaddeus's brown folder without reading their contents.

What I digested from her earlier correspondence was that she had had no luck with finding more about an adoption procedure at Gladmers Manor or a secret mistress being involved with the late squire.

Miss Philpot also had the impudence to arrive at my doorstep unannounced, but I was in bed with the flu, so Gertie brushed the nosy reporter off. Since my having health issues this winter, Gertie has become rather protective of me, and I can almost hear the stream of West country strong language that finally rebuffed Miss Philpot.

"You aint liking those letters from that newswoman, are you Mrs Lynch? Shall I ask Hermine not to deliver them anymore?" Gertie had asked with grey eyes full of concern resting on me as I lay coughing in my bed.

"No need, Gertie. They may come in useful someday." I had uttered between bouts of coughing. Gertie had asked no more but shaken her head, obviously thinking I was hiding some strange secret from her that was affecting my health. It warmed me to her even more, and I raised her pay with 5 pence a week.

This whole situation, with the uncertainty of whether to stay in Dartmond or return home, has made me run out of steam. Literally. The cold and dreary weather, the short days, the lack of my benedict's wonderful compan-ionship were too much for me. I developed a consistent cough after the flu that Doctor Suthmeer puts down to nerves.

Mind you, I don't agree with him in the least. I caught a cold while walking down Darren Street when the icy wind hit my lungs. But I was so tired from all the coughing and my lungs burning in my chest that I didn't have the strength to contradict the old-fashioned doctor.

Anyway, the good man prescribed a coughing syrup that tastes like horse dung and smells even worse, but it seems to have done the trick. I'm still weak, as my appetite has suffered even more from my illness and now, I need to get stronger to face the outside world again.

Mrs Suthmeer sent me her chicken broth, and it was as well-meant as her nosiness, but the smell alone made my stomach turn upside-down. I didn't tell her, of course, that Gertie slurped up all of it. Anyway, the broth wasn't wasted, and she's got her pan back, cleaned inside and out.

The next trouble we had was with Jasper's intestines. The poor thing had eaten something that was off or at least didn't sit well with him. Young Fritter had to almost camp here to carry the poor dog up and down the stairs at all hours.

I paid him handsomely, so the lad now has a nice bit of pocket money put aside for his American adventure, should that come to pass. Neil was the only person I saw apart from Gertie all winter, so I got to know him a bit better. Now and then he would accept a cup of tea and stay for a chat. Nice lad all around.

Fancy him not wanting to stay in Dartmond and take over his father's fish shop but leave it to his younger brother! He says he wants to emigrate to America. The young lad has quite a head on his shoulders and could have benefited from a good education. Well, I wish him luck. Young men like Neil Fritter will make their way in the world wherever they settle. Few have this knack for success, but the fishmonger's boy has it.

Anyway, it's a rather sunny Saturday morning in early April and I'm mentally preparing myself to have lived without Thaddeus for one entire circle of the seasons. I still can't fully grasp he's not here anymore, but now the veil of winter has lifted, I know what to do. Act.

After all, I hate bemoaning my state. The Good Lord has given me so much to be thankful for. I need to find a new purpose in life. Finley and Anna told me on New Year's Day to let bygones be bygones and my visit to Thaddeus's grave confirmed that. Now my health is restored, I can no longer sit here twiddling my thumbs.

"We're going home to Honeydew Mansion soon, Jasper dear. How you will love to roll in the grass again and chase rabbits in the woods." He lifts his tired head and seems to nod. I feel tons lighter expressing my wish to him.

There's a knock on the door.

"Come in."

It's Gertie, drying her hands on her apron. She's doing her brown hair up so nicely these days and her apron is always clean. The little dame will do anything to draw Neil's attention. But this time I smile. I was young once upon a time, though I never as much as chased after Thaddeus. He was the one doing the chasing. Which felt great, so I assume Young Fritter likes to see my maid making herself all pretty for him.

"What is it, Gertie? I didn't ring for you."

"No Ma'am, it's Mrs Pocock asking if you're alrite and if the kiddie can take Jasper for a walk."

"Is Mrs Pocock at the door?"

"They both are, Ma'am."

"Well, let them in, Gertie, and bring us a fresh pot of tea and some jam tarts."

"Right on, Ma'am."

Next I know, I have the first visitors to my humble abode in months. Mrs Pocock looks rather shy as she comes in, wearing a lovely mauve dress that brings out her amber eyes. I'd forgotten how nice it is to look at a pretty face and an endearing character. Timothy seems to have grown three inches since I last saw him and is almost as tall as his slight mother.

"Come in, come in. What a pleasant surprise." I rise from my chair but must grab the arm rest because I'm suddenly quite dizzy.

Mrs Pocock looks alarmed. "I'm so sorry. I heard you weren't well, Mrs Lynch. I shouldn't have come unannounced, but Timothy insisted he wanted to give you these." She pushes the boy forward, and I sink back in my chair to make sure I won't faint in front of them.

"Please sit down," I say out of breath, "I'm delighted to have some company after the months of loneliness. So please make yourself comfortable." Timothy stands in front of me with his arms behind him, an uncertain look from under a long pluck of blond hair.

"I made you this, Mrs Lynch." From behind his back, he brings out a big drawing of Jasper, which is actually well done.

"Well thank you, Timothy, that's very nice of you. To what do I owe this honour?"

"This!" He almost throws the drawing in my lap and races to Jasper's throne. The wild wagging of my darling's tail makes it clear Jasper is as delighted as his little friend. Timothy strokes the dog's head, but my Roly-Poly instantly rolls over on his back and lets his tummy be tickled. They both forget all about us.

"I'm so sorry, Mrs Lynch," the headmaster's wife says in a thin voice as she sits perched on the edge of a chair. "There was no holding Timothy back when he heard in the fish shop Jasper was ill. He kept begging me all week to come and see for himself. Honestly, he hung on Neil's sleeve every day to hear the latest about Jasper." She catches her breath. "Timothy would so much like to have a dog himself, but Mr Pocock won't have it." A sadness for her boy glides over the sweet face, and I feel for her.

"Oh, if I had known, Timothy could have come up with Neil."

"Can I come with Neil next time, Mrs Lynch?" The boy's eyes shine like burnt gold as I nod.

"Of course. I hope to go for short walks with Jasper soon now the weather is better, and my health restored, but in the meantime, if Neil has no objections, you can accompany him now and then."

"You'd better tell him when, Mrs Lynch, or he'll be at your door morning, midday and evening."

"Don't you have to go to school, Timothy?"

"Yes, Mrs Lynch. So perhaps after school?"

"Only if Neil isn't out pike fishing on the lake. You'll have to ask him."

"I will, Mrs Lynch. Thank you so much." The boy sits cross-legged near Jasper's throne and the two creatures are totally immersed in each other. I realize it's good for Jasper as well. I haven't been very good company to him lately.

Gertie comes in with the tea tray, and both Jasper and Timothy are temporarily distracted by the jam tarts. I must say they smell delicious. Gertie has just baked them, and I hope my appetite has finally returned.

As I pour the tea, Mrs Pocock asks, "So how are you doing now, Mrs Lynch?"

At that moment there is a lot of commotion outside in Darren Street and I look out of the window to see what's going on. Mrs Pocock has risen from her chair and joins me at the window. People are thronging in front of Donald's Fish Shop.

"I hope there's nothing wrong with the Fritters," I say, peering to see if I can see why people are gathering. Seconds later, Constable Columbus Walsh enters the scene. He's a big boatload of a man with enormous feet. Because of his police uniform, people make space for him, and I see him entering the shop.

"Oh, my Lord," Mrs Pocock whimpers and Timothy is by his mother's side in a flash.

"What is it, Mama?"

My years of living with a level-headed husband in moments of crisis makes me observe, "It's clearly not a health matter when the constable is called for and not the doctor. Maybe theft?"

"Maybe," Mrs Pocock agrees as she grabs her son's hand.

"Can I go and have a look, Mama? It looks so exciting."

"Fie, Timothy. Exciting is the wrong word. And no, you can't. We don't go gawking into other people's troubles."

"But Mama...?"

"Just look from here, Timothy."

When a moment later we see the new mayor, Mr Rahul Banerjee, also head towards Donald's Fish Shop, I know something serious is going on inside. As the real happening takes place out of sight, I focus my attention on the bearing of our recently installed mayor, his refined manner of dress and upright posture.

There's been so much controversy about Mr Banerjee

taking up the position of mayor here. Westminster must clearly have had a say in the matter, because despite the many protests, our half-Indian's mayor was installed in mid-February with a luke-warm reception from the Dartmonders.

Slight of build and slender-boned with a beautiful golden skin, Mr Banerjee has an exquisite, noble bearing. The way he crosses the street in a knee-length, royal-blue coat, and burgundy knickerbockers, as if he's unaware of the Dartmonders' staring at his apparel, and has just landed from another planet to set matters straight on planet Earth.

He marches to the entrance of the fish shop where people are crowding to get a glimpse. I see him raise one slender hand and the assembly parts for him to pass through.

Only a few people possess that inborn authority over other folk. It's an invisible force to which crowds react instinctively. Mr Banerjee is one of the happy few who knows how to wield this invisible power so that even the stubborn people of Dartmond are yielding to his unwanted mayorship.

I haven't made Mr Banerjee's acquaintance yet, but I'm looking forward to it. Not that I'll voice this interest left and right. Heavens, people have their hands full deciding whether they like my person. Well, that makes two of us.

Nothing happens for a while but for the growing crowd outside the shop. I decide I'll ask Neil to tell me what's going on when he comes to take Jasper out, but I'm feeling everyone's agitation and want to know what's going on.

"Look!" Timothy cries, "Constable Walsh is carrying a fish crate out of the shop."

It's true. The bulky policeman in his black helmet and black uniform holds one of Donald's wooden crates far away from his body. It is covered with a red-checked cloth. From the look on his face, Constable Walsh is disgusted with what he's carrying. He's followed closely by the mayor and Donald Fritter himself. The crowd moves with them like a flock of birds.

"The Fritter boys have probably caught a very rare type of fish," I speculate.

"But why does Officer Walch look so horrified then?" Timothy remarks observantly.

We watch as their backs disappear inside the police station next to Wilson & Son Butchers. The crowd groups itself in front of the red entrance gilded with the words Dartmoor Police Station. The people are visibly moved and upset. I know this sensation. I have seen it so often at Landdulton Police Station. It reeks of a crime discovered.

"Let's go outside and find out what's going on." I do not know where my sudden lack of restraint comes from, but my curiosity has won. I tell myself it's a fine day and I need fresh air, but really, I need to know, like all the others.

"Unless," I add, glancing at Mrs Pocock, "you'd rather we didn't?"

The flush on her cheeks tells me she's as interested as I am. Timothy is already jumping up and down like a milk punch in a shaker.

"Jasper, dear, you stay here. The mistress will be back in a minute."

My old dog wags his curly tail, gets a last pat from Timothy and we're out the door.

The pell-mell is tangible in the air as we join the crowd. Timothy is holding onto his mother's hand, a little frightened.

Mrs Suthmeer, red and flustered like one afire with wine, scurries to our side. "Have you heard? Have you heard? Oh, I need a sniff of my smelling salts. Oh, oh, my husband has been called in as well!"

"Please stay calm, Mrs Suthmeer, or you'll do yourself in." I'm more alarmed about her state of extreme agitation than of its cause, though strange, alarming words cross the air. *Dredged up. Skull. Baby.*

Mrs Suthmeer is clearly not fit to be our source of information as she gasps for air like a fish, her mouth half-open and her eyes wide. I'm glad to see our self-composed mayor step outside with the sullen-looking Walsh at one side, and the antique-looking doctor on his other. The crowd is instantly hushed as the mayor stands firmly on his elegant shoes on the wooden balustrade and clears his throat.

"My dear Dartmonders. I'm here to give you a brief statement about today's finding in Tiversack Lake. Doctor Suthmeer has just confirmed that the object that the Fritter boys fished out of the lake this morning is indeed the skull of a very young human being that's been lying in the water for a very long time. Right now, we have no sign of how it came there and why it was dredged up now. A search team under the leadership of Constable Walsh will go to the bottom of the lake to see if other evidence can be found."

At this, Mrs Suthmeer's smelling salts prove insufficient and she falls flat on her back on Darren Street. Her husband hightails to her side and brings her around. *Gosh*, I can't help thinking, *that's a bit overly dramatic,* as the mayor rounds off his morbid speech.

"Dear Dartmonders. I understand this is a horrific discovery, but please go back about your business and we'll keep you informed if there is more news."

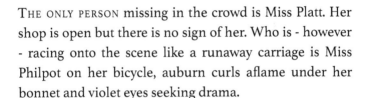

THE ONLY PERSON missing in the crowd is Miss Platt. Her shop is open but there is no sign of her. Who is - however - racing onto the scene like a runaway carriage is Miss Philpot on her bicycle, auburn curls aflame under her bonnet and violet eyes seeking drama.

6

MISS PLATT BREAKS AND I DON'T KNOW WHAT TO DO

Mrs Pocock and I look at each other over Timothy's head. Our eyes say the same without words. *This is too horrific for young ears. And we need to process this ourselves.*

The mayor disappears into the police office with Constable Walsh. Dr Suthmeer helps his wife to her feet, and she dusts off her skirts. There is an eerie silence in the crowd as everyone comes to terms with the news in their own way. The enormous question that hangs in the air is, whose baby drowned in Tiversack Lake, and when did this happen? My premonition doesn't lean towards anything good.

"I've never heard of a missing babber in Dartmond." Mrs Huckstep, the baker's wife, shakes her broad head. "If anyone should know of such a babber, it's me."

"Maybe it's a babber we weren't supposed to know 'bout," her friend and my landlord's wife, Cornelia Hopewell, chimes in.

"Maybe." Even the gossipy Mary Huckstep is lost for words.

Then the crowd parts again as if for Moses at the Red Sea. His black coat flurrying behind him and his whiskered cheeks as usual dabbed lavishly in Eau de Cologne, Vicar Foster Middlemiss whooshes past on his buckled shoes and dashes inside the police station.

"Fie, he's going to pray for the child's soul." That's the sharp voice of Miss Hermine Tow, the postmistress. "Vicar Middlemiss had better pray for his own soul. He knows I have no interest at all in his advances, but the man doesn't understand *no*." She sniffs with contempt.

I'm not completely up to date with the constant competition by Dartmond's unwed men for Miss Tow's affections, but the pretty postmistress is clearly not charmed by the scarecrow-like vicar, and I can't blame her. His Sunday sermons are eloquent and to-the-point, but the man's in need of some clothing advice and a beard-trim.

There's not much left to do standing in the street when the announcement has been made and we simply have to wait for more news. I bid Mrs Pocock and Timothy goodbye and head towards Donald's shop to see if Neil could still walk Jasper.

I pass Miss Platt's shop on my way and peer inside. All is silent and there are no customers. No sign of her either, but the blue bicycle is parked in its usual place so she must be inside.

Instinct tells me this might be the end of my search and Thaddeus was wrong about Finley's biological mother after all. If so, Miss Platt is highly unlikely to say anything now. Why would she? Nobody will ever suspect her.

As the door to Donald's shop is locked, I peer through the window. Nobody's in there, so I ring the bell.

Minnie Fritter's head shows from the window over the shop.

"Ah, it's you, Mrs Lynch. Please excuse us, I'll open the door for you."

"No need to bother, Mrs Fritter. I'm sorry."

"No, no, please wait."

A little later I hear the bolt pushed open, and the door goes ajar. I find myself in the fish shop with the tiled floor and tiled walls. Mrs Fritter looks stricken and wringing her hands, she pipes up.

"I'm so sorry, Mrs Lynch. We're all very upset. Neil, in particular. It was... it was in 'is net, you see, and the boys didn't know what it was. Thought it was an old grey ball. Do come in, Mrs Lynch, we're just having a cuppa to sort ourselves out. Would you like one, too?"

My own nerves are a little unsteady under the circumstances and, as Neil has been so kind to me and Jasper over the past months, I accept her invitation and follow her up the narrow stairs to a very similar apartment as my own.

Her husband and the two boys are seated at the dinner table, three handsome, healthy men, their caps on their knees and shuffling their stockinged feet over the rug under the table. Donald half rises to his feet in a greeting. The boys keep blowing in their steaming cups and don't look in my direction.

"I've invited Mrs Lynch for a cuppa. You will tend to Jasper later, will you, Neil?"

It looks like the young man wants to make his handsome head disappear in between his hands. He's lost his usual healthy countenance and looks distinctly unwell.

"Please don't bother about it, Neil. I'm sure I can find someone else to help me with Jasper in the coming days," I hear myself say, racking my brain how to find a new Jasper-carrier on such short notice. Well, I'll have to appeal to Gertie, if necessary.

Moist blue eyes look up at me. Through gritted teeth he mutters, "I'll do it, Mrs Lynch, no need to fuss."

"Do sit, Mrs Lynch." The fishmonger's wife pushes up an extra chair for me and I sit down at the table next to the youngest son, the lanky Alfie. A blue gaze glances sideways at me from under a dark-blond lock of hair.

"I can carry Jasper down, Mrs Lynch." There's an eagerness in Alfie's voice that reveals he's jealous of his older brother.

"No, you won't, Alf. That's my job." Neil's voice is coarse as if he's been crying, but he's clearly not going to let his younger sibling get away with his savings for his American dream. Alfie looks unhappy, focuses on his tea again.

Mrs Fritter hands me a cup of tea and offers me a thick chunk of shortbread from a tin. I dare not refuse it, but as I have no extra plate to put it on, I keep the cookie in my hand where it starts crumbling. A tiny bite from the corner tells me it's way too sugary and fatty for my taste, but I have no choice here. My embarrassment is complete as I sit with this taciturn family, who all seem to focus on my mouse bites.

"Just leave it on your saucer, Mrs Lynch, if you don't like it." Minnie Fritter comes to my rescue.

"It's not that," I protest, "it's delicious, it's just... it's just..."

"Mother, I told you Mrs Lynch doesn't eat in between meals." I'm surprised to hear Neil pitch in while the shortbread slides from my saucer on the tablecloth.

"Can I 'ave it?" Alfie's hand already reaches for the cookie.

"Don't be rude, Alfie. You've 'ad enough," his father grumbles.

"It's quite something, ain't it?" Minnie addresses me.

"I haven't heard what happened exactly, only what the mayor just told us outside the police station."

"What did Mr Benergy 'ave to say? We weren't there?" Minnie seems to be the most talkative of the family. I repeat verbatim what the mayor said and Donald nods.

"It's a bad business. Shouldn't 'ave 'appened."

I can't help putting my benedict's hat on for a moment.

"Where about in Tiversack Lake did you find... uh... what you found, Neil?" It's as if he's been waiting for me to ask. His answer comes without a hitch.

"It wasn't very far off the coast. Right in front of Gladmers Manor's boat dock. You know where the squire's family 'ave their private beach. I'd been warning Alfie we shouldn't go fishing that close to private waters, but the pike's always best there early in spring as the water is shallow and warmest in that spot."

Neil is finding his footing again, together with his tongue. He even looks at me through that curtain of strawberry-blond hair. The blue eyes still not completely dry.

"It's a bad business, Mrs Lynch. Scared both Alfie and

myself. We didn't know what to do. To throw the thing back in, or to bring it 'ome. After a second look, I could see it was a skull, so I reckoned the police would want to see it. That's why we... uh... carried it 'ome."

My mind is processing Neil's information at great speed.

"What will happen now?" I ask, not sharing what I'm thinking for fear of upsetting the family further. Plus, it's none of my business. Nothing will change in Dartmond because of what the Fritter boys brought home.

How wrong could I be?

After my visit to the Fritters, I'm back at my window, watching Miss Platt's shop. Neil has kept his promise and taken Jasper for a stroll. I think it even did the young lad some good. The colour had returned to his cheeks when he brought Jasper back in and he sat for a minute with me, telling a little more about how shocked he'd been. I really like him. He's a good boy. I'll keep an eye on him. And also on his brother. It's terrible what they had to go through today.

Jasper is snoring on his throne after devouring some soft chicken meat. It's almost six o'clock, so I expect Miss Platt to come out any minute and close her shop for the day. As far as I know, she's unaware of what happened unless Mrs Suthmeer regained enough of her strength to tell her friend the latest developments.

This whole skull story has put me off my stroke as well. Whether this is the end of the secret Christmas baby or not, I wish I had someone to share my wonderings with, but I haven't.

This will most likely be one of these unresolved issues Thaddeus and I came across a few times in this line of work, and it will continue nagging at me. There's no need to tell Finley and Anna about it; they'll find out from the papers.

Papers? I haven't seen Miss Philpot after her arrival. I'm sure she's tugging on Walsh's sleeves now for all the details. I'm also sure it will be the headline in *The Cotswolds Times* tomorrow. Will that shrewd reporter draw the same conclusions as I do? Who knows? As long as she doesn't come pestering me. Ah, I feel a migraine setting in. Too many thoughts rambling through my old head.

But there's Miss Platt. She walks slightly bent, unlike her usual swiftness. Holds her head down as if she doesn't want people to see her. I wait for her to grab the old bike, attach her bag to the back and wheel it to her cottage.

She doesn't. She seems to hesitate with the shop key in her hand. Then she walks slowly, skittishly to... the police station. She's going inside. I feel my heart thump in my throat. Why is she going into the police station? What's she doing?

Has she gone mad?

7

THAT'S THE SECRET CHRISTMAS BABY CASE UNSOLVED FOR YOU

I wait at my window until dusk at around eight, refusing Gertie's dinner of cauliflower and pork sausages. I can't stand the smell of them, though Jasper keeps promenading around my small table with his nose in the air. I don't even ring for Gertie to take the plate away.

My eyes are fixed on the red door of the police station waiting for Miss Platt to come out. She doesn't. I see the gas lamps being lit behind the barred windows. No one else has gone in or out so it's just Constable Walsh and Miss Platt in there.

I've never been inside the Dartmond police station as I have no business there, but I know, of course, what such an office looks like, having brought Thaddeus his lunch or dinner if he was working on a case that didn't permit him to come home for meals.

I'm glad to hear a rap on the door followed by Neil Fritter walking in, still looking as if he's seen a ghost but with a bit of his normal bravado.

Shall I confide in him? Or does he already know? More shopkeepers must have seen Miss Platt going in the opposite direction from home.

Let's test to see if he does.

"Any news?"

I'm not the world's best hypocrite. I can hear the tremor in my voice. He ignores my question but with his eyes on my plate and Jasper wagging his tail with might and main, Neil observes,

"Mrs Lynch, you've forgotten your dinner."

"Ah, that can wait!" I wave an impatient hand and wish Gertie had taken the plate away before I'm caught out. Caught out? I think I'm losing my wits. It is nobody else's business what I eat or don't eat.

Neil comes to stand at the window next to my chair and looks down onto the dusky Darren Street. Jasper has given up on the sausages and trots up to his side, where he leans against the young man's leg. The two have become such fit companions. Neil is a crackerjack with dogs, but then again, Jasper is a pushover for anyone's attention.

"Miss Platt's been inside the police station for the past two 'ours," Neil says in a hushed tone as if he's afraid she'll overhear him.

"So, you know? I guess the whole town knows then? What in heaven is she doing there?"

"Ah, Mrs Lynch, the gossip 'as already started. Older folk remember Miss Platt disappearing many years ago and they think it's got something to do with, you know, what Alfie and I found. The town is buzzing with theories right now."

"I see." I can't help a slight trembling of my hands, but

my voice is steady. The lad has no notion to what extent this information affects me and my abandoned search.

"I wonder what will happen next." I think aloud.

"If she's got something to do with it, she'll be locked up." Neil shrugs. He doesn't seem to be bowled over by Miss Platt's fate.

"But Miss Platt was... is such an important figure in Dartmond society. I mean, it will be a tremendous shock."

"To the old folks, perhaps, Mrs Lynch, but not to me. She's not particularly liked amongst us younger ones."

"Why's that, Neil?"

He shrugs again, "let's say she ain't fun when she organises something like for school or the church and you've got to 'elp 'er. Will pull your ear if you don't listen to 'er."

"Really?" I can't match the friendly, well-mannered Eloise Platt I met in her shop with her being cruel to children.

"I see." I'm not my usual self here, answering in monosyllables. "Well, Neil, it doesn't seem like something else is going to happen today, so just take Jasper for his last round and we'll hopefully all have a good night's rest and a brighter tomorrow."

"Yes, Mrs Lynch. Though I can tell you I'm not looking forward to fishing in that lake again. I 'eard the police will start dredging that part to see if they find more. I'm glad Dad's told me to go fishing the other side of Dartmond, but I'll never be as 'appy and carefree on the water again."

"I understand, Neil. You've had a horrible experience."

I hand him his 5p, which he pockets quickly.

"That's why I'm so grateful for these, Mrs Lynch." He taps his pocket. "The sooner I'm out of 'ere, the better."

WHEN IT'S TOTALLY dark and even the lamps in the police station are extinguished, Miss Platt's bicycle is still in front of her shop. I go to bed for a restless sleep. I'm not so much thinking of myself, but my heart goes out to the poor woman. She must have turned herself in because she believed she had something to do with the death of that child.

Which proves Thaddeus's theory that Eloise *had* a child. Whether this skull belonged to her baby or has nothing to do with her is irrelevant. She clearly believes it was her doing.

It all means Finley–if adopted at all–is not Miss Platt's son. Sir Reginald probably got the child elsewhere or maybe even fathered it with another woman.

I can continue to make plans to return to Landdulton. Finley and Anna get what they want. No closure, no consternation, no nothing.

And yet I see Miss Platt's worn features before me as if she beckons me. I do not know what this eerie feeling means, but I listen.

I ALWAYS LISTEN.

.   .   .

EARLY THE NEXT morning there is a rap on my door and Gertie introduces Junior Constable Axel Candy, who used to work for my Thaddeus at the Landdulton police station.

I'm surprised and somewhat alarmed as I haven't even finished my breakfast yet.

"Let him come in, Gertie, and serve the constable a cup of coffee."

"Yes, Ma'am."

My hands go instinctively to my hair. My night pins are still in there, but thank goodness I've taken off my cap.

In the door stands ruddy young Candy. I've known him since he was a little boy but he's far from that now. A booming six-foot-two man with a mop of red hair and keen blue eyes in a freckled, open face. A potential good officer at that, Thaddeus told me so much, but I can see that for myself.

"I'm sorry for arriving unannounced and at such an early time, Mrs Lynch." He has the Cotswold's accent but not as strongly as most.

"Not at all, Axel. I'm glad to see you. How are you and how are your parents?"

"They're well, Mrs Lynch. Mother sends her greetings, and so does Father." He stands rather forlorn on my carpet.

"Come!" I invite him to the other chair at the window and he sits stiffly in his uniform.

"What brings you here, Axel?"

It seems strange to call the grown man Constable Candy when I've always addressed him by his Christian name, and he doesn't seem to take offence. He's about to disclose the reason for his early visit when Gertie enters with the coffee. If she was a dog, she would have had her ears pricked up and I see Axel is aware of my maid's loitering around as well.

"That will be all, Gertie. Thank you."

She disappears with a sour look on her face, and I wait until I hear her dragging her feet to the kitchen. For once, her heavy tread is a bonus.

"I'm sorry to bother you so early, Mrs Lynch," Axel begins again as he stirs his coffee and keeps his eyes fixed on the cup. "We were notified by Constable Walsh of the skull that was fished up in Tiversack Lake yesterday. The place where it was found falls under Landdulton jurisdiction, you see."

The coffee is stirred, and the blue eyes rise to meet mine when he continues, "I know Constable Lynch... uh... I mean your late husband was hoping for a breakthrough in the Lowther so-called adoption case, but this seems to be the end of it. I just... I just wanted to find out how you felt about that, as your husband talked about his theories about the secret baby mystery with me so often. I also know he'd asked you to continue the work."

"That's very kind of you, Axel," I interrupt him, "and yes, I've lain awake last night because of it. Do you know Miss Eloise Platt from the haberdashery shop probably turned herself in?"

Again, the clear blue gaze searches mine. "Yes, Constable Walsh told me. It's the other reason I'm here in Dartmond. He's asked me to interrogate Miss Platt as he can't make heads nor tails of what she's saying."

"So, are you the chief constable in Landdulton now, Axel? I thought Constable Parker Parlow was chief still?"

"Oh, he is, Mrs Lynch, I'm still the assistant, but Constable Parlow has delegated this to me because I was the one discussing it with your husband." He gives me a grin as if he wants to say, *I'm not that important.* I feel sorry for young Axel because I'm sure he's twice as hard-working and three times more intelligent than that slow fox Walsh.

The gaze gauges me. He hesitates.

"Out with it, Axel. You know you can trust me."

"I know I'm crossing a moral line here, Mrs Lynch, but I'd like to work on this case with you, if you want to."

Despite myself, I laugh out loud. "There's nothing to work on anymore, Axel. At least, I don't see it. Do you?"

There's a great seriousness in the young man when he says in a low voice, "I'll interrogate Miss Platt, gently, of course, but I'd like to run by you what she says to me, if anything. I have a feeling more will come to the surface soon. Honestly, I need your help."

I don't know whether to be honoured or scared.

"Yes," I mutter, "whatever I can do."

He finishes his coffee and rises to his full length. "Can I pass by later?"

"Sure." I'm in my monosyllabic state of confusion state again, so quickly add, "By all means. Come and have lunch before you return to Landdulton."

"That would be grand, Mrs Lynch." His smile bares two rows of wonderfully strong teeth.

I PACE the room all morning, which upsets Jasper, but every time I try to sit down, I get even more nervous. It seems like Axel's interview with Miss Platt lasts hours, but finally I see him cross the street in his big leather boots and then I worry like a quivering lapdog what everyone will think seeing the constable going in and out of my door.

"She wants to talk with you," is the first thing Axel says when he's back in my sitting room.

"Me?" My voice sounds at least one octave too high. *Heavens, what now*?

"Yes, you."

"When?"

"After lunch."

I feel like shaking my head violently, like Jasper does when he's swum in Tiversack Lake. But of course, I don't show my consternation.

"And does Constable Walsh agree to that?"

"Constable Walsh couldn't care less, Mrs Lynch. He said it's my case and I can do with the woman what I want. She drives him crazy with her constant talk so he's out all afternoon, and you can go in and try to calm her."

"Is she that upset?"

"Very." Axel is adamant. "That's why I think you're the perfect person to talk with her. You know, woman to woman."

I sink back in my chair and am sure I can't eat one bite of my lunch, but I'll force myself with all my willpower. I need to be strong if I'm getting myself involved in all this. Talking about baby skulls on an empty stomach seems the most sheep-headed thing I can do.

∼

I SHIVER ALL over as I cross Darren Street with Axel marching beside me, very aware of all the prying eyes in my back. When Axel unlocks the red door to the police station, I'm ready to shout, "Nooo, let's go back!" but I don't.

It's dark and cool inside, and that specific smell I remember from Thaddeus's office. A mixture of leather, cordite and metal tang. We walk through a narrow corridor with two metal doors with small, barred windows. The police cells.

"I'll be here outside if you need anything." Axel declares.

I take a deep breath and push open the cell door. Miss Platt sits huddled in her blue coat on the bed underneath the window, her eyes big behind the gold-rimmed glasses, her bony hands gripped together as if one will never let the other go. She looks tired and worn-out but not crazy as Walsh had suggested. She nods by way of greeting.

I keep standing in the middle of the small cell, unsure if I'll sit down on the only chair.

"Sit, please." The firm voice I remember, not the voice of a broken woman.

"Are you sure you want to talk to me?" I ask in a much weaker voice than hers.

"No." The answer is honest. Then she adds, "It depends."

"Why did you go to the police station in the first place, Miss Platt?" I'm so very aware of Thaddeus's training in interrogations. He's told me so often how he went about it.

"I had to."

"But nobody suspected you of anything?"

"You did."

My mouth falls open. The woman is even smarter than I thought, but I compose myself.

"What makes you think that?"

"I know who you are. You could have only had one reason to move to Dartmond."

It seems like the roles are reversed here and I'm in the accused position.

"But you're not telling me you turned yourself in because of me, Miss Platt. Or did you fear I'd go to the police and tell them you had anything to do with yesterday's findings?"

Silence.

"But you could have denied it anyway you wanted. Nobody suspects you of anything."

"You might be wrong there, Mrs Lynch."

This makes me think. She's given something away. More people are involved. The father perhaps?

I just say "Aha," and that works.

"I wanted to be a step ahead of a prolonged search for the murderer."

The word sends an icy cold shot up my veins. Murderer? She calls herself a murderer. It takes all my effort to stay calm, and I'm glad I managed at least part of a cheese and cress sandwich.

Meanwhile, my mind works overtime. So, she had a child, murdered it, alone or with the help of others and is now afraid of justice coming from some corner.

"What have you told Constable Walsh, Miss Platt?"

"The same."

"And what did he say?"

Miss Platt laughs a cheerless laugh.

"Go home. It's not important, Miss Platt. It happened decades ago. So much water has passed under the bridge."

"So, you're free to go," I observe, "why are you still here, then?"

She hesitates for a moment.

"Mr Walsh says he'll write in his report that I'm charged with murder because I insist on it but he has no evidence to support that. So, I'm not completely innocent. And... and I'm afraid."

"Afraid of what?"

"Everything! Losing my position in society and... uh... revenge."

I nod. Everything will change for Miss Platt after this. But the revenge part intrigues me.

"Do you think I'll take revenge on you?"

She looks straight at me, no hatred, more a deep sadness.

"I know you will, Mrs Lynch. I know you cannot help yourself because of your family. You'd hoped for closure and didn't get it."

She must have gone mad after all. Why would I? My family is no longer potentially tied to that. What's she babbling about? I rise to my feet, suddenly in need of fresh air.

"I do not know what you're talking about, Miss Platt. If you know why I'm here, you also know my case is unsolved. It's other people you fear. Not me."

As I walk to the door, still befuddled by this conversation, I add, "I wish you no ill, Miss Platt. It's not your downfall or your conviction I'm after. I am... I mean, I *was* trying to solve a family issue. So, I'll leave you alone for now and hope you can restore your position in Dartmond as before. I'll return to Landdulton next month.

"Thank you for now, Mrs Lynch. I hope that will come to pass."

∼

WHEN I'M OUTSIDE, blinking against the April sunlight, I feel positively unwell. Axel grips my arm to steady me. Vaguely I realize I've been a lousy interrogator, not even asking after the origin of the child but it's too late. Through Darren Street I see a small crowd of youngsters gather; they look angry and rebellious.

"Go inside, Mrs Lynch, and stay indoors for a bit." Axel sounds quite authoritative. He returns to the police station and positions himself in front of the red door. The crowd stops at the foot of the plank way and start shouting.

"Murderess, Murderess!"

I'm temporarily glad Miss Platt is inside the police station and not at her shop or in her cottage.

While I sit in my alcove chair with a soothing cup of tea, I hear the tinkling of glass as the first window of *Treasures and Trinkets* is smashed.

∼

IT'S THEN that I realize my work isn't over yet. The case of the secret Christmas baby may remain unsolved forever but something deep inside me tells me Miss Platt is *not* the murderer of that infant but that she's protecting someone else. She has no one to defend her now.

I must have positively gone mad myself when the cage of my own prison door stands wide open, but I choose to stay.

Finding that decade-old skull so close to Gladmers Manor is just too telling to let it slip.

PART II

Case Solved

8

THE SUMMER OF MY DISCONTENT

Dartmond, Summer 1896

We're having one of those rare, glorious summers in the Cotswolds with soft rains in the night and plenty of sunshine during the day. The bluebirds and finches in the cherry tree outside my bedroom window sing as if they want to wake the dead, and the cats in the garden fight like drunks over a half empty bottle of brandy. Ah well, noisy animals are an intrinsic part of summer.

What's pleasant to the eyes and nostrils are the flowing fields of lavender just outside Dartmond. I love that delicate, sweet smell that is floral, herbal, and evergreen woodsy at the same time. It has soft, powdery, smoky notes as well. Lavender reminds me of my late mother's scented closets in Kensington.

Happy memories when life was still like shooting fish in a barrel and my greatest concern was which frock to wear to my coming-out ball.

Ah, those days are gone for good!

Jasper's been having some old-age troubles with his bladder, but for the rest there's nothing to complain about. And yet, I'm as unhappy as King Lear. We still haven't moved back to Honeydew Mansion in Landdulton but are hemmed in this rented accommodation over a bookshop with a landlord who is not only mute but downright cumbersome at times.

I mean, the paint is peeling from the walls in the kitchen and his wife just told Gertie to buy some paint and do it up herself. The audacity of these people!

Don't get me started on the Hopewells, or I'll work myself up in another frenzy.

So why didn't I do as I had promised myself and return to Honeydew Mansion? There's a reason, or rather a person, who made me decide to stay put here in Dartmond for the time being.

I'm not usually one to listen to other people's opinions unless it was, of course, my dear husband Thaddeus, but he's gone and now I have to navigate these tricky waters on my own.

I told you Miss Platt turned herself in for the murder of her baby fifty years ago, though she didn't say she did that with so many words. When Dartmond found out she had given this testimony, the town went topsy-turvy. I still can't wrap my head around it, but it was said that young Gerald Wilson, the butcher's son, had thrown a brick through Miss Platt's shop and that resulted in the town exploding like a hencoop visited by a fox.

I mean, the supposed murder took place way before most of the folk here could remember and nobody bore witness to it, and nobody but Miss Platt lost her child.

Well, there's no knowledge of who the father is, but he didn't step forward and start wielding his sword or anything of the sort.

Mayor Banerjee had a great deal of trouble talking sense back into the people, and still some of them are grumbling Miss Platt should be shipped off to Australia. People can be so vengeful for no reason at all.

Dartmond is basically split in two camps now, pro-Miss Platt and anti-Miss Platt. Most of the folk are of the opinion she can stay and just have her shop but not run her charities anymore. A small group, headed by that venomous Vicar Foster Middlemiss and Butcher Wilson, says she has to go.

And throughout this upheaval, Miss Platt is still Miss Platt, phenomenal in her own way. She still pushes that old bike up to the shop every day and disappears inside. Some of the kinder folk, like Mrs Pocock and even that gossip Mrs Suthmeer, still buy her ribbons and cotton thread and stuff. But most folk travel all the way to Land-dulton because they don't want to be her customer anymore.

I've been to her shop twice, and she's treated me as if the visit to her in the prison cell never took place. Polite, distant, friendly. I told you before, I can't read the woman, but I know there's more to this baby story than she's told so far. I might be the only one sensing it wasn't her hands to drown that baby, but who knows?

There you have it. I can't leave Dartmond yet. Maybe not even only for Miss Platt, even more for my Thaddeus. He became more tenacious than birdlime when he suspected an innocent person had turned themselves in to protect someone else. Oh yes, that happens, though not very often, and only when a case is truly sordid.

That little voice 'stay put' in my head is nagging me. There's more to come, though–by God–I do not know what. So yes, Miss Platt, enigmatic, intriguing, suspected Miss Platt has not really cast a spell over me, but has made me decide to keep an eye on her for a little while longer.

I mean, Jasper loves Neil Fritter, the fishmonger's son, whose American fortune because of my payments is growing steadily and Timothy Pocock is here every afternoon after school to play with roly-poly Jasper, who is a little less roly-poly with all the walking and playing.

It's a pleasant afternoon and I hear Saint Mary's Primary School bell ringing, so I know Timothy will rush into the door any minute. Jasper has made it a habit to lift his grizzled head and wag his tail at the sound of the school bell. I'm in my usual chair at the window, gazing down on the comings and goings of the shoppers.

Oh, there is Mrs Winnifred Herriot. She and her husband must have returned from their business trip to Chicago. How fashionable she looks in that deep-pink dress with French sleeves and an ostrich feather on her matching hat. Even her parasol is of the same colour and chintz-silk material. The sheen of it in the sunlight is enchanting.

Just the other day, I read an article in *The Daily Mail* about the Marshall Field's department store in Chicago. Glorious photographs of the lavish floors with all these women's articles, clothes, perfumes, hats, and gloves. Would absolutely be my heaven to wander through it.

I still remember as a six-year-old going to the opening of Harrods on Brompton Road in 1849 with my Mama. Old Mr Charles Henry Harrod was more into tea and groceries, but his son Charles Digby definitely had a knack for ladies' fashion. Mama bought herself some lace handkerchiefs that I've kept in their silk wrappings till this day and sometimes wear. Just a keepsake. Excellent quality of Italian damask with British lace.

Anyway, let's check what Mrs Herriot is up to, parading up and down under my window. Probably only that. Showing off her new overseas attire for everyone to admire. Oh no, there's her friend and rival, Mrs Suthmeer. My-oh-my, the doctor's wife, is dressed to the nines as well, as if it's Sunday instead of an ordinary Tuesday morning.

Heavens, Mrs Suthmeer looks almost pretty in her dark-blue dress with that aubergine shine, but her parasol doesn't match, and her hat is too pompous with all that artificial fruit on top. I wonder where they're heading.

To the Church? Oh, now I understand. Mrs Herriot's husband is no doubt the richest man in Dartmond and he's recently donated money to restore the side chapel of Trinity Church. They're going to inspect the works, no doubt, but that's hardly a reason to put on one's glad rags. I suspect the two of them are now presiding over all Miss Platt's former committees and want to give it more allure than Dartmond needs.

About that Mr Ralph Herriot. Of course, I've seen him in Church, looking all dignified in his morning coat of the best-quality beige checked wool with fashionable narrow pants creased down the front and back. He always wears coloured starched shirts with cuffs to match and white collars. And, of course, a solid tie in a matching tone. With a cane and a top hat, Mr Herriot is the best dressed Dartmonder by far. Our mayor, with his exotic colours and knee-length coats, will always be my favourite, though.

Mind you, my Thaddeus had good taste in clothing as well, but during weekdays he could only wear his police uniform. But my benedict was never extravagant or dandyish in his manner of dressing. To be honest, I don't particularly like such peacockish behaviour in a man, although Mr Banerjee is a sight for sore eyes, and I love watching him strut around Dartmond in his splendour. He's like the sun setting on the Punjab hills.

But back to Mr Herriot. It's not completely clear to me how he's made his fortune, but Herriot Lavender certainly is a competitor to Yardley these days. His manufacturing premises, where soaps, pomades and perfumes are produced, are on the outskirts of Dartmond. Most of the lavender fields are also in his possession. About half of Dartmond's adults work for him, even many unwed girls and young women.

I haven't visited the shop near the factory yet, as I steer clear of the Herriot family. Don't ask me why. I have nothing against new money, but I don't feel very comfortable in the presence of these shiny people who wave their money in front of your nose as if they can't get enough of looking at their own banknotes.

It's said they have two children as well, boys who are at boarding school. No doubt something as posh as Eton or Rugby. Anyway, that's just one of my prejudices for which the Good Lord will no doubt punish me one of these days.

Ah, there's a boy coming that I *do* like. I hear Timothy running up the stairs and Jasper is already at the door. In another year, Timothy will be able to carry Jasper down. That will be a suitable replacement for Neil Fritter, who talks about leaving for New York next summer.

9

HOW TIMOTHY POCOCK BRIGHTENS
MY AFTERNOONS

"Mrs Lynch! Mrs Lynch, do you know what I heard?"

That boy is so loud but also so lively. He makes my old heart enjoy life a little more.

"No Timothy, I haven't heard. Pray, tell me. Look, Gertie's put your lemonade ready for you and some biscuits for you and Jasper."

For a moment, the ten-year-old with the spiky blond hair and brown eyes is too absorbed in slurping down his drink and sharing his biscuits with Jasper. My two sweet-toothed lads, I call them.

Sitting cross-legged on the floor with Jasper showing his white belly to be tickled, Timothy blows the tuft of hair from his eyes and looks up at me.

"Mother told me that Miss Platt is going to close her shop."

An involuntary tremor goes through me. Is business that bad for the poor woman?

"Oh," I reply, "that's a sad business."

Still caressing Jasper, Timothy, who's a bit of an old soul, says contemplatively,

"Exactly what I told Mother, Mrs Lynch. I mean, it's not good that she killed a baby, but she's not in prison or anything. I don't think she would kill another one, do you?"

I inwardly chuckle at the boy's logic, but don't show it.

"No, I think that if it happened, it was more of an accident. Miss Platt is not a criminal." No need to tell the boy I have a hunch she wasn't even involved in it.

"Some people like Gerald Wilson think she is a baby serial killer. He says naughty words about her, like "witch" and "gun for hire."

"Fie, Timothy, I don't want you to use these words in my house."

"Sorry, Mrs Lynch." He looks guilt-ridden. "I just thought that you wanted to know these things, as you're always so interested in everything about Miss Platt."

This makes me sit up. If a small whippersnapper like Timothy Pocock is aware of my focus on Miss Platt, it's probably obvious to everyone.

I defend myself by saying, "It's not that, Timothy. We were all upset this spring and since then, things haven't really calmed down around Miss Platt, have they?"

He focuses his wise-beyond-his-years eyes on me as if trying to read my mind. Then he says slowly, "I just thought that because Mr Lynch was a policeman, you would be a bit of a policewoman yourself."

"Good guessing, young man. Shall I tell you about one case I helped solve for my husband?" His eyes light up with excitement, very much a ten-year-old again.

"Oh yes? Really?"

Now I wonder if it's a wise decision to introduce such a young one to the ways of the law, but there's no backing out.

"I want to be a policeman when I grow up." He confides.

This makes me smile. Which boy doesn't dream of that? I fear his parents want him to pursue an academic career, but I won't spoil his dream for him.

For once, Timothy abandons Jasper to sit in the other armchair at my window. All readiness for my story in his school uniform and grazed knees. With a pang, I realize this will be the closest I'll ever come to a son or grandson.

"All right." I'm raking my brains for a story that won't upset his young mind and find it in the love story of Miss Phoebe Hewlett.

"There was this young farmer's son in Landdulton, Nathaniel Horgan. He lived with his parents on a farm just outside the town, well-to-do farmers, but not the richest in the area. One day Nathaniel would inherit the property, as he was the only son, but also a handsome amount of money. Of course, Nathaniel's parents wanted him to marry into one of the best families in the neighbourhood. They'd let their eye fall on Miss Phoebe Hewlett, the daughter of a rich but peculiar scientist, whose estate was next to that of the Horgans."

Timothy shows impatience, as he crosses and uncrosses his bare legs like a grown man. Most likely imitating his father, but the expression on his young, freckled face clearly states he has no interest in the background of this story and only wants the gory details. But that's not how I tell a story.

"I don't know if the young couple themselves had any

say in the matter of their partner's choice, but probably not. In those circles, it was still the parents who decided. So, one day in December 1890, the parents announced Nathaniel and Phoebe's engagement with an eye to a great Christmas gathering of both families." I drop my voice a little to keep Timothy's attention.

"But in the week after the announcement, Phoebe goes missing. Great consternation in Landdulton, even in the entire Cotswolds. Of course, my husband was called in and as it concerned a young girl, he asked me to accompany him, should we find her. Now there had been young girls missing in the 1840s, all of whom got murdered. All except one, Miss Eloise Platt. But that was forty-five years before Miss Phoebe's disappearance."

Timothy pricks up his ears, wants to ask a question, but closes his mouth as he folds his hands in his lap. I see I have his full attention now.

"Yes, it was a terrible day because everyone was reminded of those missing girls. Three of them missing in the Spring and only Miss Platt in the autumn, more or less like Phoebe. But could the unknown murderer have struck again after so many years? It seemed unlikely, but you never know.

"No matter how far and wide the police force searched–and the days were so short that they ran out of time–they couldn't find her. Even her husband-to-be, Nathaniel Horgan, joined in the search. We were all so worried.

"So, one day, there was a drizzly rain and a leaden sky. You couldn't tell the difference between the water and the sky as we were trudging along the shores of Tiversack

Lake. At some point, Nathaniel comes up to me and asks if he can tell me something. I say, *of course.*"

Timothy is now hanging on my words, so I draw out the story a little.

"Nathaniel is all flustered and anxious, so I ask him to speak up, but he's waiting until the others are out of earshot. Then he whispers, 'Do you know Miss Phoebe Hewlett, Mrs Lynch?' 'Of course,' I reply. Now you must know, Timothy, that Miss Phoebe was quite a character and was very set in her ways. I think her parents mainly steered her towards this marriage because she was so wilful and independent.

'I'm in a real pickle, Mrs Lynch,' the flustered Nathaniel continued, 'because... uh... I know where Miss Phoebe is.'

"I remember stopping there right in my tracks, pricking my parasol in the wet sand, and looking up into that young fellow's face with considerable anger. I mean, here we are at least fifty people looking for the damsel for days, and all the time her beau knows where she is?

"'I'm so sorry, Mrs Lynch,' Nathaniel stuttered. 'I'm willing to go to prison for this. The thing is, I don't want to marry Phoebe, and she doesn't want to marry me. I promised to help her escape to London and give her some time to get there before she was dragged back home. I'm... I'm in love with Hildred Hunter, the vicar's daughter.'

"'Stop right there, Nathaniel,' I ordered him and blew the whistle Mr Lynch had given me to draw attention when we'd found something."

I stop to look at Timothy, who gazes at me in astonishment. "What happened to Nathaniel and Phoebe, Mrs Lynch?"

"What do you think, Timothy?"

"I think they were forced to marry, after all. That's what I would have decided."

I smile at the boy's righteousness but shake my head.

"No, their respective parents were forced to pay a considerable compensation for all the police work that had been done for nought. But as both the Horgans and the Hewletts had deep pockets, it didn't really hurt them. Nathaniel got to marry his Hildred and Phoebe was wise never to return to Landdulton so as not to be cut to pieces. As far as I've heard, she lived with an aunt in London until she got married to some Marquis last year. And that's the end of my story."

"Do you still do police work, Mrs Lynch?"

I shake my head. It's no use explaining to this young boy why I'm here. Not that I know myself anymore whether I'm still doing my investigation. If Miss Platt closes her shop, that will be the end of keeping an eye on her. A little voice in my head whispers, *You'd given up on your search, hadn't you?*

"Time to go home and do your homework, Timothy. Your parents will wonder what keeps you so long."

But the shrewd young man isn't done yet.

"Do you think we have to help Miss Platt, Mrs Lynch?"

I sigh rather deeply. It's exactly what I've been thinking.

"How would we do that, Timothy?"

"I'll ask my mother. She always says Miss Platt did so much for Saint Mary's Primary School and also for

Trinity Church, and so... Maybe it's time we do something back for her? I mean, I don't think she should be punished in this way."

"You're a wise little fellow, Timothy Pocock, but as long as Dartmond is divided over this issue, I don't think that whatever we attempt to undertake will really restore Miss Platt's place in society."

Timothy gets up from the chair, a profound frown on his freckled forehead. In a grown-up voice, I'm sure also his father's, he announces, "Leave it with me, Mrs Lynch."

Heavens, the boy's such a delight. He gives me these inside chuckles he knows nothing about.

"Bye, Timothy."

"Bye, Mrs Lynch. Bye, Jasper."

10

THOSE THINGS I MUST CONSIDER
BEFORE I ACT

W hen Timothy's gone and while I'm waiting for Neil to take Jasper out, I ponder a little on how to proceed. As I already said earlier, there was a good reason to stay in Dartmond for the time being to keep Miss Platt in my vision.

When she was still in the police station, I had another visit from that reporter, the libertine Theresa Philpot, who has been scribbling all sorts of tidbits about the old case and the new case. Miss Platt's disappearance in 1845 and her recent confession were all over *The Cotswolds Times*. As if there was no other news in the world. I thought it all rather overdramatic, but the readers gobble her columns up like custard pies, of course.

The violet-eyed lady also told me casually that there are no adoption reports on Dartmond or Landdulton from the 1840s. And that no Dartmond unwed mother had given birth to a child except for a Mildred Godkim.

There's a fire in that newswoman that would even

ignite wet wood. I must simply keep her at an arm's length. She wondered aloud and, in my presence, why I wasn't going home yet. As if it is any of her business where I choose to reside! Theresa Philpot may be smart. She's also a bit of a nuisance. Sorry to say it. I remember my benedict commenting on her figurative enormous nose. Ah, well, she's probably the best reporter the local newspaper has, and there's something to say for that. Well, I dutifully cut out her articles and add them to Thaddeus's brown file.

That Miss Philpot! She insisted on me calling her Theresa, which I found unheard of. Can you imagine? I've only associated with her once. Of course, I rejected that proposal. She's Miss Philpot to me and that's it.

But as you may have gathered from my earlier ramblings, I appreciate intelligence, whether in a male or a female. I don't distinguish there. So, she had an interesting theory about Miss Platt, which is underpinned by my friend Constable Candy and my own misgivings about Miss Platt's testimony.

Miss Philpot argued that the fact that Miss Platt confessed so readily to the murder of her child, within hours after the skull being fished out of Tiversack Lake and nobody accusing her of anything, is suspicious. Certainly, if she kept the murder secret for fifty years, clearly no one suspected her of anything. Miss Theresa's exact wording was "this is fishy," which I found a bit of a pun, but as the reporter carried a severely serious look on her well-formed face, I didn't think it my place to make a quirky remark.

With a deadpan facial expression, which I'm sure still

displayed the laughing wrinkles near my eyes, perhaps even around my lips, I asked Miss Philpot: "So what do you think Miss Platt is hiding?"

To which the good woman replied, "The truth, of course, Mrs Lynch, nothing but the truth. Nobody can prove Miss Platt had even anything to do with that skull. Some folks may remember she disappeared and came back to Dartmond and we have my father's clippings, but that's all we know of the facts."

I can tell you that Miss Philpot had me intrigued further by this notion that Miss Platt must have a motive to confess to a murder nobody knew about and that no one could ever convict her of due to lack of proof, but my brain gets muddled wondering why she would do such a thing. I mean, what would she be hiding that is worse than confessing to the murder of your own baby?

This happens in this line of work and why I think I'm not really cut out for it. You have the stone-cold facts and evidence: Miss Platt disappeared for three months in the 1840s. Fifty years later, a baby's skull is found in Tiversack Lake. Then you have the more confusing facts: Miss Platt declares the baby's skull was from her baby, that it is her fault, but doesn't want to give any further details about how it ended up in the lake nor how she got pregnant in the first place. I mean, we could probably pressure her further to get the truth out of her, but I doubt whether that would help make sense of things.

Miss Philpot, of course, is just a nosy reporter with too much time on her hands and a dash of self-invented human psychology up her sleeve. She throws out this theory that nobody can prove, but that sounds like there may be a trace of evidence. Any self-respecting dog might wish to sniff out that route. And so does the empty-handed detective.

But then there's also young Assistant Constable Axel, having informed me that Miss Platt showed strange behaviour during his interrogation. According to him, she was one moment emotional and teary, and the next minute aloof and vague. But what he found most striking was that there were several moments where she clearly hesitated before answering his questions, searching for her words, spinning her thoughts. When he would press her further to clarify things, she'd refuse to answer, claiming her memory failed her.

Hadn't I had the same experience with her? It was odd in the first place that she'd requested me to come to her cell and then given me next to nothing in return. She just hadn't been confused or emotional with me. So, was that a ploy she had used on the policemen? But not on me?

And now she's closing her shop, whether because she has not enough customers, feels threatened, or can't face society anymore, God only knows. I have a strong inkling, though, that she needs to be kept in business.

I'm not afraid she'll do herself in or run away. Though one can never tell with folk under pressure. It's more that I can't bear her silent suffering, simmering day in and day out without making a clean sweep with the truth.

I mean, what must it be like to make an entire town believe you killed your own child but don't have to go to prison for it? Or had she wanted to stay in jail, but Constable Walsh didn't want to keep her there because it was too much work for him? Oh, all these endless, unanswered questions!

When I'm really honest with myself, though, I've set my heart on knowing the truth. It's even beyond my promise to my benedict. It's like a personal pursuit now.

I ring the bell cord and wait for Gertie's heavy footsteps. Jasper raises his sleepy head from his red-velvet cushion, clearly communicating he doesn't feel it's time to go out yet. What a lazy dog he's become, but he gets enough exercise with Neil, so I don't blame him.

"My summer coat and hat please, Gertie."

"Will you be out long, Ma'am?" The maid's blushing cheeks tell me she hopes I'll still be out when Neil drops by.

"I don't know," I answer honestly, "I hope Mayor Banerjee will have time for me."

"Mr Benergy? Are you sure, Ma'am? I 'eard he was out of town?"

"Now where did you hear that, Gertie?"

"Miss Hermine told me this morn' when I collected your mail."

"Good gracious!" I can't help exclaiming, now I've got a plan, and it is thwarted when I'm all doffed up in my summer coat, hat, and lace gloves. Gertie is clearly troubled. I never lose my patience, no matter how gladly I would snap at her sometimes.

"Oh, it's nothing you've done or not done, dear Gertie. I was just... uh... I am in great need of Mr Banerjee."

"Of Mr Benergy, Ma'am? Are you 'aving trouble with the Hopewells again? I can deal with that for you." The puzzlement now cascades from my fretful maid's features. I realize a call for the need of the mayor must seem like an emergency. Certainly, because I didn't announce it in the morning.

"No, silly Gertie, nothing like that happened. But it's sweet of you to offer help. It's just an old case my husband was involved in before he passed."

I could've bitten my tongue off there and then. What made me blurt out that? Now she'll think I'm on to something. But to my surprise, Gertie's face lights up.

"Oh, yes, Ma'am, of course. Well, I 'ope Mr Benergy 'as arrived back from 'is earlier business."

"I'll try to be back before Neil comes, but should he be early, don't keep him from his fishmonger business."

I can't help myself, though I know I'm hopeless at keeping these two lovebirds apart. *Nature.* I sigh as I make my way down the narrow staircase. Nature *will rise like oil to the fore.*

The first person I encounter as I walk out my front door and open my parasol is my landlord, Richard Hopewell. He's arranging the newspapers in front of his shop with his back to me, so I hope to slip past him unnoticed. Alas, he turns and beckons me into the shop with an urgent wave of his spidery hand.

Now, don't get me wrong, Mr Hopewell is a perfectly normal human being, not even bad looking in his late sixties, with a healthy countenance and not an ounce of extra flesh on his tall posture. Even a thick crop of silver hair on his head. Neatly dressed in a suit and tie, as always. It's just the fact he doesn't talk and that he has these big, watery green eyes under silver eyebrows holding an expression as if he's just seen the devil jump naked into Tiversack Lake. As if the world doesn't make much sense to him.

I think, "Oh Lord, what now?" But I can't simply ignore him and walk away. He may be mute, but he's not deaf or blind.

I follow him into the book and stationery shop, dragging my feet as slow as molasses in January. As expected, his wife Cornelia stands ready behind the counter to word her husband's desires. Now here's another specimen of a woman that–let me put it mildly–I have many reserves about. It's not her outward appearance - well-dressed, well-mannered, always smiling–that unsettles me.

Like her husband, she's in her sixties, but it doesn't show. Few lines in her face and just a few grey hairs in her wavy blonde, wavy hair. A certain distinction. But I'm not sure what's on the inside of Cornelia Hopewell. She keeps that well hidden from the world.

My Thaddeus always said you can read a person's character in the position of their mouth. According to him, as soon as they stopped smiling, the corners of their mouths would drop into disdain. And he's probably right, as he usually was. Mrs Hopewell's smile is certainly of that kind.

"Mrs Hopewell," I begin in badly faked chirpiness, "how are you?"

"I'm well, Mrs Lynch. Thank you. I hope you are, too."

Spill the beans, Ma'am, I think, as I have difficulty keeping the corners of my own mouth turned upwards.

"I don't know if you've heard the latest news that Miss Platt is closing her shop?"

Gracious God, is it everywhere?

"Yes, I've heard." I give up all pretence at being benign. It's no use.

"So, my husband and I thought that perhaps, seeing that Miss Platt has no heirs, we could buy the shop and maybe you could turn it into living quarters for yourself? We know the upstairs apartment is not really up to your standing."

Not only do I lose my smile, I almost lose my manners. How dare she? It's not her shop. Miss Platt isn't even gone, and she's already forging plans.

"Is my presence in your rented accommodation no longer wanted?" One of my eyebrows goes up, and there and then I decide I'm going to rent the ugly place for as long as I can.

"Oh no, no, no." Cornelia exchanges a quick glance with her husband. "On the contrary. It was meant as a sign of goodwill. You'll have more space and Jasper will be downstairs."

"Is Miss Platt's shop for sale?"

"It will be." Cornelia Hopewell raises her hands as if saying, *I've concocted it altogether with our Lord and Master so don't worry about the details.*

"Maybe if she sells it, another haberdasher will want to continue *Treasures and Trinkets*?" I can't help proffering that option.

"But who, Mrs Lynch, who?" It's all organized in Cornelia's mind, and she looks at me as if I'm a simpleton.

"I'll think about it when it comes to pass," is all I master to answer, murmuring under my breath, "which will be never when I have a say in the matter." Then louder I add,

"I bid you good day."

First nodding to Cornelia and then to Richard, I leave the shop as fast as my legs will carry me. Never ever will I buy a red folder or anything in that shop if I can help it. I keep up my pace in the direction of the mayor's office. It's even more important now that I speak with Mr Banerjee.

11

A MOST PLEASANT GENTLEMAN
AND A POTENTIAL ALLY

"Leeches, they're just leeches," I keep repeating as I swiftly advance through the blue door that has in golden lettering *Dartmond Town Hall* above it. But a small part of my mind worries that I'm trying to keep a protective hand above the head of a potential criminal. It's just that Miss Platt and murder seem as far apart as the North and South Pole.

Inside the town hall, a clerk is sitting at a desk, bent over a large ledger in which he's scribbling. The young man looks up when I come in and I'm struck by his intense blue eyes set rather closely together. They shine like two sapphires in an otherwise bland face.

"Yes?" he asks, but then returns to his writing.

"Is Mr Banerjee in, by any chance? I'm Mrs Lynch, the widow of Chief Constable Thaddeus Lynch from Landdulton, and I'd like to see the mayor."

I don't know why I add my background information in the mix, but the young man seems so disinterested in my nearly-out-of-breath arrival that I feel I must throw some weight behind my request.

"Mr Benergy?" The sparkly eyes look at me as if the lad's never heard of our mayor. He even repeats, "Mr Benergy?" But then he slowly rises from his desk and, smearing his ink smudged fingers on his not very clean pantaloons, makes for the back door.

"Let me see if he's here, Mrs... uh...?"

"Lynch. Mrs Imogene Lynch."

Heavens, what an ignoramus!

He returns, blue eyes and all, and points to the door he's just come from.

"Mr Benergy can see you now, Mrs Lunch."

Rolling my eyes, a tad too crabby, I enter Mr Banerjee's office and am instantly at ease. It is as if I'm entering a temple, not that I've ever seen one, but what I imagine it would look like. The room smells of delicious herbs I can't identify, but there is also a touch of lavender and thyme in the air.

And then the colours, warm earthy tones - yellows, orange and reds - large brown sprawling furniture and folding screens delicately painted with birds of paradise and laid in with ivory. Two large fans cool the room.

I'm so taken by the atmosphere in the room that I almost jump when, from behind one screen, Mr Banerjee's melodious voice calls me.

"Mrs Lynch, are you there?"

Before I can say 'yes', the slightly built mayor in his many-hued garments appears from behind the screen with his slender hand outstretched. His handshake is strong and warm. The brown eyes are even warmer. Exquisite black hair and whiskers.

I'm bereft of speech, not a state I usually find myself in, but then again, I've never been close to a half-Indian gentleman before, so forgive my clumsiness.

Mr Banerjee doesn't seem to mind my unforthcoming behaviour–he's probably all too used to people gawking at him with their mouths open. Instead, he gestures to two large wicker fauteuils with their carved lion heads and colourful cushions in the middle of the room.

"Do sit, Mrs Lynch. I've been meaning to make your acquaintance for some time, but work has kept me so busy. I'm therefore delighted you've come yourself and very glad that I have a spare moment for us to be conversant with each other."

His English is perfect, straight out of Oxford, and his manners absolutely high-class British. It suddenly pops into my mind that Mrs Pocock told me that Mr Rahul Banerjee was born and raised in England, with an English mother and an Indian father.

"Let me take your coat and hat, Mrs Lynch." I've already taken them off and he goes over to the coat rack to hang them up. Then he rings a tinkling bell.

"Coffee, tea, a refreshment?"

"Tea will be fine, thank you."

I sit down in the comfortable chair and watch how the mayor sits down opposite me, not slouching but very erect without using the back cushion in the chair. From the glass-panelled coffee table, with lion heads as feet, he takes a box with thin cigars and lights one. The blue smoke whirls upwards and the aroma of tobacco, leather, wood, old library books, and spice mesmerizes me further.

Fie, take a hold on yourself, Imogene, I scold myself

inwardly, but it isn't often that I'm swept off my feet like this.

"So, what is it you wanted to discuss with me, Mr Banerjee?" I'm still Thaddeus's wife and will not be knocked out of my wits for long. At that moment, the clerk stumbles inside with the tea tray, and I wonder if Mr Banerjee and he are the only two people working in the town hall. Well, it's none of my business.

The tea tray lands safely on the table, with the tea still inside the pot and the cups, though askew on the saucers, not broken.

"Thank you, Hardy. I will serve Mrs Lynch her tea." And to me the mayor adds, "Have you met my right-hand Hardy Crowle, you know, Mr Leonard Crowle's eldest?"

"Please to meet you, Hardy," I say, racking my brain to determine if I knew the undertaker had a son.

When Hardy is gone and we're both sipping our Darjeeling tea, that delicious vegetal, mossy, fruity, and citrus taste, the mayor answers my earlier question.

"I've made it my first assignment as the Dartmond mayor to become acquainted with my citizens, whether they've lived here all their lives, or settled in more recently."

Mr Banerjee smiles that wondrous smile of his that is hard not to be mesmerized by.

"The last category only had one name in it, a widow from Landdulton. Now don't get me wrong, Mrs Lynch, but this piqued my interest because I couldn't find any of your relatives living in this town, which–curious creature that I am–made me wonder why you settled here in widowhood."

Taking another deliberate sip from his tea, he pauses

and then looks at me with those friendly, dark eyes that glitter as if containing an undisclosed mischief. It is clear from his glance that he's already got his answer, but wants to hear it from my mouth. Before I can answer him, he continues, however, in an almost conspiratorial tone.

"Don't think I've been questioning your motives, dear Mrs Lynch. That would have been inappropriate from my side."

I smile back, feeling at ease for the very first time since I became a Dartmond resident. In these foreign surroundings with this well-mannered, kind gentleman, it is as if I'm stripped of all my former worries and concerns. Like traveling to an unknown resort, where one can replenish the soul and return home rejuvenated.

His next pause shows he is awaiting an answer, but not in a hurry. At that moment, I get a hint at what Mr Banerjee's magic is. In his presence, it is as if all time stands still. As if the hands on God's big clock move at a snail's pace and the present moment is all that matters.

"My move to Dartmond is the exact reason I came to visit you today, Sir." I clear my throat and then add quickly before I'll regret it, "It has everything to do with Miss Eloise Platt."

The mayor nods, a quick movement that makes his goatee go up and down with a funny little jump. The dark eyes rest on me but without pressure.

And then I tell him the entire story and how I think Miss Platt is not a murderer and should be saved from the vengeance of some Dartmonders until the truth comes out. Maybe offer her money to keep her shop open. When I'm done, Mr Banerjee taps the slender tips of his fingers together, which makes his golden pinky ring with a huge emerald flash in the afternoon sunlight.

"Aha," he finally says and then again, "Aha. I know it's a preposterous assumption, Mrs Lynch, but I had hoped that we could be friends."

I feel myself frowning. Friends? What is he talking about? Has he now lost his sophistication? And it's exactly what I reply.

"Friends?"

He waves an apologetic hand, "Oh, I'm so sorry, please forgive me. I used the wrong word. I should have said associates or perhaps allies. I had no intention of offending you, Mrs Lynch. You do know I hold you in high esteem?"

He is not mocking me, but Mr Banerjee doesn't strike me as a man who chooses his words out of his hat, so I'm still confused. And a little flattered.

"Forget my assumption," he says with another golden smile. "Let's just say I'd hoped you'd tell me the whole messy business, Mrs Lynch, but I'm well aware of all the delicacies in this sad matter."

"I do not know what you know and don't know, Mr Banerjee." I sit up a little straighter in the comfortable chair.

The tapping of the fingers stops, and he picks up the cigar that was smouldering in the ashtray's corner. How I like these manly habits and how I've missed them. Though Thaddeus was more of a pipe smoker, a man and his tobacco belong together. Though I care little for men who smoke cigarettes, especially more than is needed. Through the smoke, my host continues.

"Let me see. I've spoken to both Constable Walsh and

Constable Candy. They've let me read the reports on Miss Platt they'd written. And Constable Candy told me there is a file in your possession compiled by your late husband." He says the word 'husband,' softly, as if afraid the word will hurt me, which it always does a little, so I appreciate the care he takes.

"I've had an interview with Miss Philpot from *The Cotswolds Times*," He smiles rather roguishly, as if saying *what a character she is*! "The interview was officially to write an article on me in my function as the new mayor, but..." Here he chuckles, a rippling sort of laughter that comes from deep in his throat. "... but I turned it around because of the recent upheaval with the findings in Tiversack Lake. As you know yourself, Miss Philpot doesn't mince her words. So, I can say I know a fair deal, but am interested in what you could contribute."

"Aha." I seem to have taken a subscription on that word this afternoon. Well, I become monosyllabic when asked to be forthright. First, I'm not Miss Philpot, I don't wear my heart on my sleeve and second, I find it hard to speak my mind when I haven't hypothesized a situation for myself.

It's not that I don't trust the man opposite me, or wouldn't want to get his help, it's this tangle about what to do or not to do in my head.

Mr Banerjee clearly reads my silence as unwillingness and quickly adds, "Forget my request, Mrs Lynch. I'm such a bore only to talk about Miss Platt with you when it is much more interesting to get to know you."

Before he changes the subject, I quickly interject.

"No, no. I will tell you. I came here specifically for Miss Platt's situation. I need your help, so I'm very grateful that you offer it. Have you heard that the Hopewells want to buy her shop?"

A thunderous cloud passes over the mayor's dark features.

"I have, and I can tell you I'm not happy with it. Miss Platt's family has had *Treasures and Trinkets* since the beginning of the century; her grandfather Bernard Platt opened it in 1802. But more importantly, Dartmond needs a haberdashery shop, as much as it needs the Hopewells' bookshop."

One cannot help but be impressed by the speed with which the mayor has accustomed himself to the ins and outs of his community.

"I agree," I say, "it's the very reason I wanted to discuss this matter with you, Mr Banerjee. I wonder if we could come to some arrangement so that Miss Platt can keep her shop, at least temporarily."

I can't tell the good man yet that I want to investigate the whole skull story further, so I quickly add. "I'm willing to contribute to such a plan from my own means."

Now it's the mayor's time to say "Aha." As if he's glad he finally gets a glimpse behind my façade, but quick as the snap of a finger he leans forwards over the coffee table and whispers.

"Is the reason for your generosity that you have additional reason to presume Miss Eloise Platt is hiding something else from us?"

His question comes down on me like a bolt from the blue, but I bounce back the next second. Heavens, this man is sharper than the law allows.

"Do you believe she is?"

The warm smile returns and his coffee-brown eyes light up.

"Oh, yes."

"It is wicked of you to think that is funny." I can hardly suppress a smile myself. Associates, he'd said, allies. Friends is out of the question. Males and females cannot be friends in my opinion. Unless they are wed.

Mr Banerjee jumps up from his chair as if he suddenly remembers he's left the kettle on.

"Dear Mrs Lynch, it's been an absolute pleasure, but duty calls. I will see that a secret fund is raised to support the continuation of *Treasures and Trinkets,* and I look forward to your contribution. As soon as the details are ready, I'll ask Hardy to pass it by you. In the meantime, I hope you will drop by here whenever you feel like it."

He almost waltzes around the coffee table to shake my hand firmly. "Do keep in touch, please. People like you are what makes my occupation wonderful."

As he darts to my coat and hat, I say to his slender back, "thank you, Mr Banerjee. I will."

When I'm back in the street, I feel slightly dotty. As if my hat is askew on my head, but when I feel for it, it seems to be all right. This is not who I am and how I behave.

I shake my head, but giggle inside.

12

AN EMERGENCY THAT CHANGES EVERYTHING

W hen I get back in the door and heave myself up these awful stairs, Gertie is standing on the landing, wringing her hands, and looking in a tizzy. It immediately changes my good mood.

"What is it, Gertie? Is it Jasper?"

"No, Ma'am, Jasper is fine. It's Miss 'ermine Tow. She says you must come to the post office immediately. I didn't know what kept you so long. There's a telegram from Gladmers Manor."

"A telegram? Heavens." I immediately turn around to go downstairs again.

"Do you want me to come with you, Ma'am?" Gertie's voice is tiny as a mouse.

I'm moved by her kindness and swear I'll be nicer to her.

"No, no need, dear. I'll be back in less than no time. Best put the kettle on."

"I will, Ma'am."

Momentarily, I don't know what to think or feel while I rush across the street to the post office. People only send telegrams when there are bad tidings. But I force myself to stay calm and not expect the worst.

Dear Imogene, do not anticipate trouble, or worry about what may never happen.

Keep in the sunlight. That's my Thaddeus helping me to remember one of his favourite Benjamin Franklin quotes. If one of the founding fathers of the United States spoke such wise words, why should I worry about a mere telegram? Even so, I don't have the stature of men like Franklin or my benedict. Women are different.

Women are tougher! My benedict again. I nod my head to his wisdom, realizing people in the street must think me daft as a brush.

I push open the panelled door to the post office with such vehemence that the bell attached to it clangs for dear life. Pretty Miss Hermine Tow, who's flipping through an illustrated magazine, jumps up from her chair as if death warmed up.

Caught you red-handed, I think, but do not say.

"Mrs Lynch, oh yes, your telegram. Let me get it for you."

"As you most probably already gobbled up its contents, you might as well tell me what it says," I murmur under my breath. Miss Tow, her hips swinging a mite too provocatively under her deep red frock, glides to the back of her office. I don't have time to tell you all I think and do not think about Hermine Tow at this moment, but I will at some point. Don't worry. For now, I'm focused on that message.

Miss Tow returns with the dark-yellow, flimsy paper and hands it to me.

"I hope it isn't a sorrowful message, Mrs Lynch."

"It probably is," I say rather curtly, as I tuck the post office telegraph away. I'm not giving her the joy of seeing me read it here.

"Good luck, Mrs Lynch! And goodbye." No wonder men fall for that honeyed voice; she'd have done well as a Greek Siren, the alluring miss.

"Thank you. I'm sure Gertie will fill you in on the details." I can't help myself. I know I'm a nosy person myself and will probably be punished for it in the after-life, but it's still my duty to set some standards here for these young chickens.

The telegram burns in my hand, but I decide I need to cup of tea before I can open it.

Finley had a heart attack. Not life-threat-ening. In Landdulton hospital. Love, Anna.

I CLASP my hand over my mouth as I read Anna's words over and over. They make a kind of rhythm in my head. Three three-words sentences and one with two words.

The Wedgwood cup clatters on the saucer when I put it back. Then I inspect the clock around my neck. Four p.m. Too late to travel to Landdulton now, but I'll ask Gertie to order the coach for tomorrow morning.

Then I sit and think. What a weird day it's been.

Certainly, a day in which the Lord had a big hand. I feel that my visit to the mayor and this telegram are somehow connected. Connected to the lady who is putting Final Sale signs next to her items in her three shop windows.

For the past year, I've felt like I am in a limbo. Nothing seemed to move, at least not in the direction I wanted to and now, with Finley's life in danger–no matter what Anna claims–everything seems to spread like a flock of geese in the winter skies. I have to get at the truth of Finley's parentage. Regardless of if he tries to persuade himself that he doesn't want to know. In his heart of hearts he must want to know the truth as badly as I want to know it. It even pushes my preoccupation with Miss Platt's story to the background.

My promise to Thaddeus becomes more urgent now as well. What if Finley dies? If only he'd taken more care of restraining his appetite. Hopefully, the doctors will put him on a diet now. All that roast beef, port wine and apple crumble can't be good for the body.

Which brings me to the notion I haven't eaten since breakfast. I sigh. No wonder I feel low. I ring the bell cord vigorously. If Finley's going to die from eating his way to a heart attack, I run a risk of wasting away eating air. Fie, Imogene! If only Thaddeus were here. He always got me eating, the dear one.

$\sim$

NEXT THING I KNOW, my carriage is rolling along Tiversack Lake to Landdulton's hospital in bright summer sunlight. With the misanthropic Jack Cadden on the box, I needn't fear interruption of my thoughts, which is just as well, as I slept badly and have a slight headache.

The journey is uneventful and summery. The light pains me and I pull my summer hat deeper over my eyes. Seeing my cousin ill is not something I look forward to. He and I may not be incredibly close, but he's dear to me, and the only family I've got left. At least in the country. Cousin Catherine still seems obsessed with her pyramids in Egypt.

I see Catherine's face before me, very similar features to her late father, my Uncle Reginald, and her aunt, my mother Heloise Lowther. Long, lean, elegant faces with fair hair and big, deep green eyes.

Very unlike Finley, it's true. He also doesn't resemble the photograph Catherine showed me of her mother, my Aunt Kittie, the one in the asylum whom I've never seen. If she's still alive. Makes one wonder if Uncle Reginald told the truth on his deathbed. Does Finley resemble Miss Platt? It would take some imagining seeing a likeness there, but it's closer than to the Lowthers.

Oh, but Finley can't be her child. Or is he and the skull had nothing to do with either of them? How my poor head throbs. Finley can only be Miss Platt's child if she lied about the skull being from her baby. But why should she? What has she to hide? I know Mr Banerjee also suspects she's cloaking the truth. Anyway, I've gone down that dead-end street too often already.

I focus my attention on Catherine again. Somehow, thoughts of my energetic cousin go well with summer. I've always been fond of her, looked up to her as a child. She's three years my senior, but with that exuberant character and that unbreakable belief in herself, quite a different temperament. Young Catherine is Katrina Garbert-Smithe all over again, my mother used to say. That is, before Aunt Kittie fell ill.

ACCORDING TO MY MAMA, Katrina, or Kittie, was the life of any party–and she threw many. Lady Kittie was also the belle of the ball and a great communicator. The pinnacle of extroversion. Another of my mother's labels. Perhaps a little on the wild side, but very much adored by everyone she came in contact with. Uncle Reginald was besotted with her, as he was with his daughter.

Yes, everything must have changed after Finley's birth or arrival at Gladmers Manor. Mind you, I still loved the summers with my mother in the Cotswolds. It was our annual treat away from bustling London, plenty of space and all these fun out-of-door activities, horse-riding and summer fairs and picnics at the Lake. But there was always that sadness present.

My mother filled the role of mistress of the house because Aunt Kittie was in the hospital. I don't know if Uncle Reginald ever wanted to remarry. He stayed a married bachelor for the rest of his life.

I've never given the matter much thought, but I suddenly remember rumours about Sir Reginald Lowther not really being a ladies' man. Whatever that means. But happy? No, he wasn't happy, and neither was Finley as a young man. Not until he married Anna Lynch. Only Catherine escaped the Gladmers' gloom and doom.

After her brief marriage to that long-faced, long-limbed scientist Ulysses Pandy, she went globetrotting and only came on fleeting visits to the place of her youth. I think I've seen her three times in the past thirty-five years.

"We're here, Ma'am." Cadden pulls the horses to a stop, and I glance up at the red-brick building of Parkview Hospital. Not a place I look forward to entering again. Poor, poor Thaddeus. At least he was discharged to pass quietly at home. Oh, I so hate this place and the way it smells. *But, in you go, Imogene, no more dilly dallying.*

As I'm making my way to the nurses' office to ask for Finley's room, someone calls my name. I turn around to see my former doctor and friend, Ed Rule, coming towards me with his hands outstretched.

"Imogene, so glad to catch you. Your cousin has just been discharged. Minor heart attack. He can rest further at home. Is your carriage still here?"

"Yes, no worries, Ed. Oh, that's good news."

It's always good to see our loyal doctor, and I shake his hand warmly. Ed was my prop and stay during Thaddeus's long illness. I always say Dr Rule talks with his hands, not with his mouth. He utters these short staccato sentences as if they have no relation to one another. But he's a fine man, not bad-looking either for being past fifty, in his pin-striped suit and bowler hat.

Has an adorable wife, too. Julietta, some Greek or Italian roots there. I fondly remember our card game evenings during the long winters. Punch and cheese crackers and much laughter.

"Thought you'd rather not be here, Imogene. I'll walk you to your carriage. Do visit us when you have time. Julietta misses you."

"So thoughtful of you, Ed. And yes, I will. I've just

been busy in Dartmond." I feel myself resorting to short sentences as well.

"Well, hope to see you soon, Imogene."

"Bye, Ed. Extend my greetings to Julietta. I promise I'll visit you both soon!"

As I wave to the good doctor, I give Cadden instructions to take me to Gladmers Manor.

FINLEY LIES PROPPED up on a heap of cushions on a bed in one of the Lowthers' many living rooms, his pallor ashen but smoking a cigarette. One of his hunting dogs lies on a rug in front of the bed. The windows are open and the warm summer sun streams in.

Somewhere a gardener is snipping the hedges. It all looks quite peaceful and normal except for Finley in a bed, his rather prominent belly protruding through his navy silk pyjamas. It smells of cigarette smoke mingled with the fresh scent of the lilies of the valley in a vase on the table.

"Ah cousin Imogene, you shouldn't have bothered to come so soon. See, I'm right as rain."

"Of course I had to, Finley. What a shock you gave me."

Anna enters the room with a pillbox and a glass of water. "I heard you had arrived, Imogene. How lovely of you to make the effort."

As usual, we don't shake hands, but I take off my hat and summer coat and sit down at Finley's bedside.

It is silent for a long minute. That awkward silence

that seems to hang between us oftentimes. Thankfully, Anna breaks the ice.

"According to Doctor Rule, Finley should just take it easy and go on a diet." Finley groans, showing his discontent at this prospect, but Anna continues in her normal level-headed way, "It'll do you good, Finley. You always complain you can't keep up with Efry Galway when you go hunting in Hungry Summit Hills. Or go for a walk with the dogs, for that matter. Soon you will do both."

"I'd rather eat my partridges than shoot them these days, but it's true, cousin. Doctor Rule has told me to tighten my waist strap. Ah well, I'll do my best."

"I'm sorry," is all I can offer.

"It's made me think, though," Finley adds, "when you're not sure if the moment has come, you're going to meet your Maker. It changes one's perspective. As I was lying there in Landdulton Hospital last night and couldn't sleep, I started thinking about what my father told me on his deathbed, and I said to myself, Finley old chap, do you or don't you want to know the truth about your birth? I mean, the money's long paid to that Foundling's Hospital. It's more for myself now."

He stops, looks from me to his wife. Anna sits straighter. She's a Lynch, after all, and knows how much her brother fought to get every crime or mystery solved. Not that we know if a crime was committed in Finley's case. I hold my tongue, waiting for him to continue.

"I know I told you to drop the search on New Year's Day, Imogene. And after it was clear Miss Platt couldn't be my mother, you know, the whole skull business, I thought I'd come to terms with it. But last night it really started gnawing at me. It's just, it's just that we're at a dead-end, aren't we? I mean, if it had been Miss Platt, I'd been thinking of offering her some compensation, after all. But what am I to do now?"

"Don't worry, Finley. Worrying will do your health no good," I say, feeling a gush of relief that he's at least open to get at the truth, if we ever get at it.

"If you want to find out whether you're a born-Lowther, I'll leave no stone unturned to discover your origins. I'll start by talking things through once again with Constable Candy. He's such a smart officer. And the new Dartmond mayor has also offered his assistance."

"Isn't that the Indian mayor?" Anna asks with apparent shock in her voice. I feel like I have to defend Mr Banerjee.

"He's half-Indian. Only looks it a bit, but he's a fine English gentleman."

"I couldn't care if he was a Creole." Finley laughs out loud. "Heavens, we're so uptight in this country."

"Fie, Finley." Anna is clearly not amused by her husband's radical thoughts. Finley only laughs again and lights another cigarette.

"You shouldn't smoke so much, dear," Anna scolds him.

"If I can't eat, I must smoke, or I'll die of misery, anyway."

I feel as if the heart attack has caused a change in Finley's character. He seems freer, ready to jump at a second chance. But Anna is at a loss about what's happening here. They were such a team in holding up their defences of society, and now she sees that defence crumbling. It's not like I'm a freethinker myself, but these two could benefit from being a little less uptight. If Finley sets the tone, Anna will follow.

After a coffee and a thin slice of bread, I ramble back in the coach towards Dartmond. I'll catch Axel when he has his Wednesday meeting with Walsh and ask him to come and see me.

For the rest, I'm back at square one. Only now, with Finley's longing to know who he really is.

13

A MAD DASH FOR THE TRUTH

Dartmond, October 1896

Two more months have passed and I'm not one inch nearer to the truth of the secret Christmas baby. As the trees are casting off their leaves, and the swallows are migrating southwards, I'm feeling as useless as a gun without a trigger, time-passing and ruminating.

Finley is restored to good health and indeed seems to make an effort at controlling his appetite.

The fund raised by Mr Banerjee has kept Miss Platt in her shop, though not without some protest from her side, and the general mood of tranquillity reigns once again over Dartmond. Miss Platt's critics now hold their tongues, at least with the mayor publicly supporting her.

Jasper is healthy, Neil and Gertie are officially courting each other, and I'm still in my cramped surroundings over Hopewell's shop inspecting the comings and goings of whoever passes my window.

Mrs Peaton is still presiding over Honeydew Mansion for me, but I don't know for how much longer.

Everything in the world seems in order.

My official period of mourning is over, so I sometimes allow myself to wear colour - mostly pale blues, and moss greens. They've always been my favourites. But if you know me a little by now, you realize that all this upbeat talk is only to conceal the fact that I'm far from happy.

I think–by now–I'm the only one seeking closure on this fifty-one-year-old saga, if that's what I may call it. Even Finley, marching up and down Hungry Summit Hills with his pal Ephraim Galway or his hunting dogs, and a much slimmer figure, doesn't seem to mind his origins anymore.

Still, there's a glimmer of hope and from a very odd corner. A dream. I hardly ever dream of Thaddeus, no matter how I pray for a glimpse of him from the other side, but a couple of nights ago, he was suddenly there. He must have sensed my despair because he said to me,

"Imogene, dearest, you *will* solve this. I know you will."

"But how, Thaddeus?" I was almost crying in my sleep, which was awful because I wanted to be so happy that I was finally seeing my benedict.

"Wind back the thread to your past, Imogene. Think deeply. There's one knot you haven't untangled yet." And then he'd disappeared, just as I thought I was going to get an answer.

So, as I watch Mr Crowle study the Victoria Sponge and the Madeira cakes in Huckstep's shop window, almost with his nose against the glass, I brood on the meaning of my dream over my cup of tea. What's in my past? What's the knot? What's the jumble?

Jasper's intestines are playing up again, and I put my hanky over my nose. I love my roly-poly dearly, but wish he'd smell like the daisies. Well, he doesn't.

Who said that? *I wish my dogs smelled like the daisies.* And then added, *Well, actually he does. Daisies smell awful.*

Who said that?

It is as if I'm dreaming while awake. I hear laughter and see sunlight flicker through the foliage. I'm lying on a picnic blanket with my mother next to me. But there's someone else. My mother laughs out loud. "You have the funniest expressions, Kittie. You should be a novelist."

KITTIE! Aunt Kittie.

IT CAN'T BE. I never met her. She was hospitalized soon after my birth. Did my mother visit her in the asylum? Took me with her? Oh, I can't ask Mama anymore. I wish I could.

But here's the forgotten piece in the puzzle, the forgotten everything by everyone. Why didn't I think of Aunt Kittie as a person, a witness before? I feel like God is wrenching my heart out of my body for cruelness. I don't even know if she's still alive. She's probably long gone. She would be in her eighties by now.

I've never heard of anyone ever visiting her. I can't remember my mother ever talking about her sister-in-law. If we visited her, I must have been very young.

Finley never even as much as mentioned her. Still, I

read the 1846 clipping from *The Cotswolds Times* that announced Lady Kittie Lowther's admittance to Ridgeview Asylum. It was important enough at the time to mention it in the papers. Her last mention. Then eternal silence.

"I'm not to blame, God!" I protest aloud. "I was only a couple of weeks old when she was sent to the hospital." But then I add, "you're a sloppy DC and an even worse family member, Imogene!"

Did Thaddeus take her into account? There's no record of that either.

The last question and answer must have actually left my mouth aloud because Jasper tilts his old head and says 'woof' once. Now despite Jack Russells being terrible barkers, my darling hardly ever makes a sound so this must mean something.

Was this what Thaddeus tried to tell me in that dream? To unravel this last knot? To find out if Aunt Kittie is still alive and might be sane enough to tell me something? Or even why she was packed away and never heard of again? Or am I now really going mad as a hatter, putting two and two together where there is none.

To be honest, I'm a little disappointed in Mr Banerjee. I'd hoped he'd be more forthright in his assistance, but his intention was clearly only to set up the secret fund.

Speaking of which... there's our mayor going down Darren Street. Let's see where he's heading. Ah, I thought so. Miss Platt's shop.

Now, shall I cross the street and just casually drop in for some bobbin cotton? One button of my coat is loose. I curb my curiosity and decide I'd better go to the post office and send a telegram to Miss Theresa Philpot. She's the only one I can think of who can do the research and find out if Lady Kittie Lowther is still alive and at Ridgeview Asylum. Isn't it odd that I should have to ask the nosy reporter to help me, after all? I just don't know who else to consult. That's it.

On my way to the post office, I almost bump into Mr Banerjee, whose visit to Miss Platt's shop must have been a brief one. He tips the side of his white summer hat.

"Mrs Lynch, so good to see you. I'd hoped you'd pay me another visit after we rescued our Dartmond haberdasher shop."

"Good afternoon, Mr Banerjee."

I'm tempted to tell him what I'm about to do but bite my tongue just in time. It's most likely a loose end, so why rock the boat before the storm hits? I smile as we shake hands and I feel the strength and warmth of his touch like the first time.

"I'm glad my money has come to good use. Miss Platt also has more customers." I say kindly.There's that golden smile again.

"I'd hope you'd keep an eye on that, Mrs Lynch. I wondered. It was what I wanted to discuss with Miss Platt, not in detail, of course, but how business is faring as she was so set against our plan at first. But she was busy with a fitting for a waistcoat for Dr Suthmeer so I told her I'll come back another time."

He smiles at me again from under his white hat. "Which means I have a free half hour. Would you care for Darjeeling tea, Mrs Lynch?"

I'm about to say, 'no thank you' and proceed towards the post office, but before I can say it, my mouth has already spoken. "That would be delightful."

Pudding-head! I scold myself for reacting on a whim and thus interfering with my plan. But when we're seated in the colonial chairs in that magnificent office with the sweet-scented tea, I know I needed this break. The room relaxes me, and Mr Banerjee's energy is mysteriously soothing to me.

"I may have a clue."

Oh, that blabbermouth of mine. I don't know what's come over me, but since the dream and since thinking of Aunt Kittie, I'm as rudderless as a drifting ship.

Mr Banerjee, clad in a long, embroidered black coat with buttons down the front and white linen trousers, sits up even more.

"Please tell me, Mrs Lynch. I've been praying for a breakthrough. Though we've put step one–keeping Miss Platt in business–into operation, we're no closer to the truth."

I nod. Exactly my thought. And before I can stop it, I hear myself say,

"Just this afternoon I realized I haven't investigated if Lady Katrina Lowther is still alive."

Mr Banerjee interrupts me. "Is that the lady in one of the clippings? The one who was admitted to Ridgeview Asylum?"

Another nod on my behalf. The mayor puts his cup and his cigar down to tap his fingers together.

"You might be on to something there, Mrs Lynch. I happen to know the current head of Ridgeview Asylum. Doctor Alexander Alardice. He's the son of Doctor Jennings Alardice, who was mentioned in the article. Why didn't I think of this before?"

"You know him?"

I don't know whether to be pleased or to become alarmed.

"Yes, we're both on the Board of the Bristol Royal Infirmary. I meet him once a year, so it's not like the doctor is in my inner circle." He looks pensive for a while, the dark brows knitted.

"But could you send him a message, perhaps?" My voice sounds doubtful.

"I think you would have had noticed if she'd passed," the mayor thinks out loud. "It's a known fact that people with mental illnesses but an otherwise robust constitution can become very old. As long as their routine is the same day in, day out."

"Oh," I reply rather sheepishly, "but then it might not be a good idea to talk to her, should she still be in Ridgeview Asylum."

It's so good to speak my troubled mind and share my thoughts with someone sympathetic and willing to think along. At this moment, I'm very grateful for Mr Banerjee's presence.

"You know what, let me first find out if Doctor Alardice can affirm Lady Lowther is still alive. I can make that phone call right away from the post office. Miss 'Eavesdropping' Tow is out and the Postmaster General never listens in on conversations."

My heart makes a little jump. "Would you? Oh, Mr Banerjee, you are just like me. Make hay as the sun is shining." A chuckle escapes my throat.

"Exactly, Mrs Lynch." The mayor jumps from his chair like a light-footed cat. "Please pour yourself another tea. I'll be back in the wink of an eye."

My heart is racing when the mayor is gone and yet

through all the turmoil, I find myself praying that Aunt Kittie is alive and able to talk. Whatever she may remember, or not. And who knows, maybe she would enjoy my visit and I can amend a wrong that has existed in my family for far too long.

But when Mr Banerjee races back into the room, his face is sombre, and I fear the worst.

"The good news is that Lady Lowther is alive. The bad news is that she's very frail and confused. Doctor Alardice did say that you can visit her. He was actually surprised someone was interested in her, but he does not know how she will react to a visitor, as she's never had one. Oh, and she's bedridden. Has been for over a year now. 'A fragile greenhouse plant.' The doctor's words, not mine."

I let the news sink in.

"What now?" The words are spoken before I realize it.

The mayor's eyes shine with that golden-brown light.

"Well, Mrs Lynch, you know the answer to that question. Nothing will stop you from the truth, so I'd say, hire that carriage and go over to Ridgeview Asylum." He stops, takes a drag on his cigar. "Don't think I don't appreciate this is the hardest thing you've had to do so far, dear Madam. I know. But I also know you're the only one who has the temerity to see this through."

I take heart from his words.

"All right. I'll visit the asylum."

14

MORE ANSWERS THAN I CARE TO GET

Ridgeview Asylum lies at the foot of Hungry Summit Hills just east of Landdulton. At first sight, it's not very different from an ordinary hospital, a three-storey building in red stone with many windows. The differences lie in that the building hides in the woods and is surrounded by a high fence. All the windows also have bars in front of them, which makes it look like a prison.

Thaddeus and I have passed the road along Ridgeview often, but I've never been this close to the gates. Jack Cadden was at first obstinate that he didn't want to take me there, but lavish payment always changes the coach driver's mind.

He reins in the horses, and I descend from the coach to ring the bell that is attached to the porch in the fence. I instruct Jack. "Wait for me here. I won't be over two hours."

"That'll take my whole day," the morose man grumbles.

"I've paid you for a whole day, so just take a nap at my expense." I only snap at people when I'm tired or nervous. Meanwhile, a nurse in a wide white cap and a white apron over a long black dress has come to the fence.

"I've come to visit Mrs Katrina Lowther." My voice sounds way too thin and high.

But the nurse smiles and unlocks the heavy metal padlock and lets me through.

"You must be Mrs Lynch. Doctor Alardice told me someone had called to visit the Lady. That's what we all call her here." The way she says 'the Lady' sounds affectionate. It eases some of my disquiet that my aunt has been locked away in a draughty cellar with only a dry piece of bread per day.

"How... how is she?" I stumble over my words as my cheeks redden. The neglect is most likely all mine and not this institute's.

"Hard to say, Mrs Lynch. She goes up and down all the time. Doctor Alardice has recently increased her laudanum dose, and first we had the idea that it helped, but yesterday she had a very bad day. We feared it would be her last. Eating is a problem as well, so we feed her porridge and soup. She has no teeth left and her eyesight is very bad as well. Mind you, for an eighty-one-year-old, she's not in a poor condition but after she fell last year and broke her hip, she's been declining. We've tried to get her out of bed, think she could still do that, but she refuses. I'm so sorry for talking so much." The nurse looks rather timidly at me.

"No, please, I want to hear everything before I see

her." And then I can't help myself and blurt out, "I'm so very sorry I didn't come earlier. I... I feel terrible."

"Oh no, Mrs Lynch, don't fret. We see that all the time. Hardly any of our patients get visitors. They're just no longer part of this world. All they have for comfort is us - the doctors, the nurses, and the chaplains. No one cares about these poor creatures. No one." There is some fierceness in the nurse's words. It doesn't make me feel better, but I'm sure she doesn't mean it that way.

"Is there anything else I need to know?" We have meanwhile arrived at the front door, which the nurse opens with a latch key and then quickly locks behind us.

"Just be yourself."

Like most of you, I suppose, I'd never entered an asylum before and I thought I'd be confronted with people hanging onto my sleeves and hems, hollering in empty hallways, and being kept in rein by doctors in white coats.

Well, Ridgeview Asylum isn't anything like that on this October afternoon I am visiting it. The hallways are serene and white, music from a piano sounds from behind one of the oak doors and someone is banging along on a xylophone. It smells of tomato soup and fried onions, not an unpleasant smell, and through the open windows I see people working in the gardens, bent over flower and vegetable beds.

The nurse who is accompanying me seems to pick up on my surprise at the calm and general well-being the place radiates.

"Doctor Alexander Alardice and his father Dr Alardice Sr, who's still on the board, run this place as a large household. As Matron, Doctor Alardice's wife,

Mildred, is also deeply involved in the care for our patients. They lovingly call her Aunt Millie. Ridgeview Asylum is inspired by the pioneering work of Doctor William Charles Ellis at Hanwell Asylum."

I listen intently, fascinated. I mean, I've been living near this hospital for decades and have never even known this to be such a modern facility. The nurse, meanwhile, takes the stairs to the first floor and I follow her as she continues to instruct me.

"Just like Doctor Ellis, we believe in what he called, 'the great principle of therapeutic employment'. Work, combined with religion, is essential for patient recovery and rehabilitation. Your aunt, for example, worked in the kitchen for many, many years and became quite a chef. She's famous here in Ridgeview for her cranberry pie, which now goes by the name of Lady Pie. When she's very low and unhappy, one of our patients will bake her pie and, lo-and-behold, she'll always nibble on a slice and smile her toothless smile. It's a sight for sore eyes, I can tell you, Mrs Lynch."

The love expressed for my poor aunt touches me deeply, to the extent that when we arrive at what most likely is her bedroom door, I put my hand on the nurse's sleeve and swallow with difficulty.

"I'm... I'm so incredibly grateful to you all for taking such great care of my Aunt Kittie. Please tell me, is there anything I can do in return?"

The nurse, who still hasn't told me her name, smiles from under her white cap. She has light-blue eyes with many creases around them in a kind, round face.

"I'm just grateful you've taken the effort to come, Mrs Lynch. As I said before, most people shun this place. It makes us often feel our work is only for God and the patients. Of course, I know who you are. Your husband was a renowned constable here in the Cotswolds and your reputation as his prop and stay has also come to our ears.

"I'm Dora Grain, head nurse. Anytime you'd like to become a volunteer or even take a seat on the Board, you're very welcome, Mrs Lynch. Just let me or Doctor or Mrs Alardice know. I could see if one of them has a moment for you after you've visited your aunt. Just to make each other's acquaintance?"

"That... that would be wonderful." I hesitate and then add, "Will I be on my own with my aunt? What if... you know... something happens that is out of control?" I hate asking this, but Nurse Grain laughs heartily at my worries.

"You'll both be fine, Mrs Lynch. One of the staff checks in on her every thirty minutes, so you won't be alone for long. And I'd say visit with her for only an hour. It will tire her too much."

"All right." I take a deep breath and push open the oak door. The room is dusky, the flower-patterned curtains half drawn but I can make out a single bed, a washstand, an old-fashioned armoire, and a small table with sweet-smelling tea roses on it. What strikes me most is that the room is painted in bright yellow, which makes the walls jump at me as if I'm standing in a sunflower field in mid-summer.

"Is that you, Maddy?" a croaky voice demands from under the same floral-patterned quilt as the curtains. I don't know what to say; my tongue is glued to my palate until the voice calls out with more authority, "Maddy, do come closer, you know my eyes are poor. Why are you teasing me?"

"I'm... I'm not Maddy," I stammer, inching towards the bed.

"Who are you then? I don't recognise your voice. You sound London-like, just like Heloise."

"Heloise?" My voice falters even more. "You mean Heloise Bowditch?"

"No, silly. I mean Heloise Lowther." The figure moves in the bed, turns to me. "Come here. Let me have a look at you."

I do as I'm bid, feeling more like a ten-year-old than a fifty-year-old. The woman in the bed has remarkable features, is very strong and very prominent. She's old all right, her mouth sunken because of the loss of teeth, but her eyes burn with a bright-blue light as two sapphires in the sun's glitter and her skin is still taut over her high cheekbones. Only the fallen mouth has wrinkles around it.

There's no doubt that Aunt Kittie must have been an absolute beauty in her youth, and I instantly recognize Cousin Catherine's prominent features and blue glare.

"You are there, Heloise? What took you so long?" she lisps. My Aunt lifts her head from the embroidered pillow and stretches out a bony hand layered with thin skin and thick blue veins. The hand that grips mine is strong and pulls me closer. "Let me have a look at you. Oh, these darn curtains, can you open them? My eyesight is so poor."

I still have difficulty moving as I'm so moved inside. Here's a very alive person who is not the unsound mind I had assumed she would be.

"I will open the curtains for you," I stammer but she keeps holding my hand, peering in the dusk with these glittering eyes.

"You're not Heloise! Who are you? What are you doing in my room?"

"I'm... I'm Imogene, Heloise's daughter. You're my Aunt Kittie." I'm almost crying as I say it, but then she lets go of my hand.

"Now do open that curtain, child, I'm all confused here."

I comply with her instructions before returning to the bed where another order awaits me.

"Put these cushions in my back so I can sit up a little. Imogene, you say? Imogene?"

As I help her sit up and help her thin back in the pink nightdress rest in the cushions I smell her, a combination of rosewater soap and old age but not unpleasant. There is still a certain cleanliness about her. "Now get me my glasses. They must be on the side table or in the drawer. I still can't see you properly."

I'm so out of sorts I can't find her glasses though they're right in front of me.

"Here you go," I say with a timidness I don't recognize in myself. When Aunt Kittie is finally installed with glasses and cushions, she observes, "Now sit very close to me on this chair, child, so I can have a good look at you. If you are who you say you are, you're my niece, but I only saw you as a baby, so you must forgive me. I don't immediately recognize an old woman."

This makes me laugh despite myself. Yes, the spirit is there all right, just like in my cousin. An old woman, huh? Well, I guess, I am just that.

"I'd like some tea now and wouldn't mind a piece of Lady Pie. I'm quite upset."

I agree she looks a bit out of sorts, squeezing the floral quilt between her fingers and rolling her eyes from me to the door and then to the window.

"Can I ring a bell, or how does it work here?" I want to make her feel more comfortable, and tea would help me as well.

"You go to the kitchen and get it. That's how it works, child."

"All right, but where do I find the kitchen?"

She fixes me with the glittering gaze.

"Are you a bit squirrelly, perhaps? You don't know where the kitchen is? If you're trying to fool me, child, you have the wrong person. Now get us some tea."

"Sure. I'll be back in a minute."

"You do that. I'm not going anywhere."

Hoping to find a staff member in the corridor to point out the kitchen to me, I am glad to see Nurse Grain coming my way carrying a tray with a teapot and the requested pie. I smile in relief.

"How did you know?" I ask as I take the tray from her.

Nurse Grain gives me a wink. "We know because we care."

Aunt Kittie has her eyes closed with her glasses hanging halfway across her face when I come back into the room with the tray. I fear she's fallen asleep and decide to wait with pouring her tea. But then she says in that croaky voice with her eyes still closed and the glasses askew,

"Why are you not pouring the tea? It will get cold, missy!"

"Sorry, I thought you'd fallen asleep."

"You are really a bit soft in the head." She opens her eyes again, but smiles when I put the cup and saucer on her bedside table and add the sugar.

While she sips her tea and sucks on her pie, a thought wrinkle appears on her forehead. The glasses are still not in place. Then she bangs the cup on the saucer and says, spouting a spray of crumbs, "So why are you here, Imogene?"

A clear question, no beating around the bush, not one degree of mental illness. She just doesn't look at me but closes her eyes again.

I know I need to talk but I feel so tongue-tied. All I can do is to be honest with her and tell her how I feel about having neglected her all these years.

"Aunt Kittie, I'm so sorry I haven't come earlier." There, it's said.

One eye opens and fixes me.

"Balderdash!" she croaks and then laughs out loud. Not condescendingly, but rather merrily. "Let me tell you one thing, Imogene Bowditch. I've long forgiven my family. I'm happy here. I have people around me that really care for me, so cut your gibberish and get on with it."

Nobody in life has ever made me feel like such a bad person as I'm feeling right now. She is right. She is honest.

But then I find some of my strength back and say, "I will tell you why I'm here if you agree to me visiting you again."

"Have I ever stopped you from coming?" The glasses go in place on her nose, and she resumes her tea drinking. She seems disinterested in me, so I wait and drink my tea.

This woman is quite something, remarkable and sharp. I wonder, deeply wonder, why she is here in the first place and feel terribly uncertain about broaching the topic I came for. Was there a secret in the Lowther family that led to Aunt Kittie being locked away? Was it against her will?

I sigh. I wish nothing of this had ever happened but then I hear myself start, first tentatively and then with more determination. Everything from my marriage to Thaddeus and Anna's marriage to Finley, to her late husband's declaration to Thaddeus before he passed. I just don't tell her about Miss Platt and the baby skull.

When I'm done, I sit still with my hands folded in my lap. I am sending up a silent prayer to the Lord. Aunt Kittie is silent as well. She's actually lying so still that I again think she's fallen asleep. But then she stirs with her eyes closed.

"Imogene, Imogene!" she croaks, "you're not to blame. So, stop troubling yourself. Finley's not to blame either. Nor are my daughter or Heloise. How could you know? I don't even blame Reginald. I *was* ill when I came here. Have been for a very long time. It's just the care and the work and the chaplains have helped me become another person. A person I like. And then I didn't want to go anywhere else anymore. The doctors would probably have let me go but I was happy here. I have friends here that are like family. I've had a good life, so don't you fret."

"But why did you never ask for us to visit you, Aunt Kittie?"

She laughs again, out loud and merrily. "Oh child,

family don't want to visit someone in an insane asylum, you know that."

"But that's because they don't know that it's..." I falter.

"Quite normal?" Aunt Kittie laughs.

"Well, I'm very glad I came," I say with conviction.

The blue eyes fix me; a dark cloud veils them for a moment.

"Beware of what you're saying, child. The truth is ugly. Uglier than you can imagine."

A shiver runs down my spine at her words, and I gasp for breath.

But Aunt Kittie laughs again, "you said your husband was a constable, and you helped him many times. And that Reginald got cold feet before he had to face his Maker. You know, Imogene, I wish he hadn't because it would not have overturned any apple carts and we would've never had to meet. You may think you are frightened by the truth, but I lived it and I'm not looking forward to returning to that dark place again." She's very serious now.

"Then please don't, Aunt Kittie. It's not worth it. I'm sure that if my husband had known there was so much grief involved in all of this, he wouldn't have wanted me poking around in it. Please don't upset yourself on my behalf."

The eyes close again and the bony fingers squeeze the quilt with the dots of cranberry pie. The wrinkle returns on her forehead.

"I don't know everything, Imogene, because as I said, I was very ill at the time and mostly in my room. I am talking about the autumn of 1845. But I did hear bits and pieces and I will share them with you. Not that I know if they will be of any use to you. And after I've told you, you must find a nurse or a doctor for me because I will need my laudanum. If you're serious about wanting to visit me again, you may–but I don't know if I'll be around much longer. The dear staff here wants me to hang onto life, but I'm actually almost ready to go."

She stops, her eyes are permanently closed now so I can't see how she feels.

"I will do as you tell me, Aunt Kittie, and I will be back soon. I promise."

There's a strange longing in her voice when she says, "Will you bring Catherine? She's the only one I'd love to see again before I go."

Tears start dripping down my cheeks and my voice is quite hushed when I say, "I will try to find her, Aunt Kittie. Last I heard, she was in Egypt doing some archaeology research, so it may be a while before she's back in England."

"Never mind then. I just thought I'd ask."

"I'll send her a telegram. I promise."

"All right. Listen up, Imogene Bowditch. Eloise Platt came to Gladmers Manor sometime in October. I don't know how she arrived there, but I know Reginald took her in. And she was pregnant, but I do not know who the father was. I am sure it wasn't Reginald's child." Aunt Kittie stops to take a breath.

"After Catherine was born, I had had my first mental breakdown. The doctors told me this was a condition that was most likely to return when I had another child. I was feeling so ill at the time, I never wanted another child, but as you know we had no son, so there was no heir.

Reginald didn't mind not lying with me. He was interested in men, not in women, if you know what I mean."

Again, that laughter, as if there is no sorrow in her heart anymore, but a second later my aunt dives into gloom again. The frailty of her health becomes more apparent to me.

"Anyway, at some point, Reginald must have come up with a plan. Eloise Platt couldn't keep her child because she was unwed and probably had fled her family, and there was a possibility she'd have a boy. We could adopt it and because I was never in society, nobody would suspect it wasn't our legitimate son. You can't blame the man under the circumstances, and I suppose Eloise Platt was also content with this arrangement. Reginald had a doctor come specifically from London, so no local doctor was involved. I heard that doctor's voice, you know. Not a local man.

"I stayed out of sight all the time. Catherine was my pride and joy, and I spent as much time together with her when I felt well enough. So, a lot of what happened at Gladmers in those months leading up to Christmas is guesswork for me."

She stops for a moment, turns on her side with her face away from me. I don't know if I must make a sound to let her know I'm still here and listening. She resumes her tale.

"There was a lot of fuss on Christmas Eve. It must have been the time of the delivery. I was quite unwell but had lunch with Catherine, who went back to the nursery with her nanny. A French girl, I think it was. Catherine was very fond of her. Emilie or Odille. We had two and don't know which one it was.

"Then strangely enough, I felt much better on Christmas Day. It was a fine day. A friendly sun and no wind, so I told the nanny I wanted to go for a walk along Tiversack Lake with Catherine. Just a short walk, only fifteen minutes because I was so quickly tired. I don't know where Reginald was. We had little contact at the time, which was fine. Ours wasn't a love relationship. Catherine was holding my hand and skipping by my side. And then... then..."

"What is it, Aunt Kittie?" I feel my throat squeeze tight.

"It was Eloise Platt. She was wading into the lake in a white nightdress, looking very pale. She was holding what looked like a baby in a blanket as she was going under water." Aunt Kittie's breath wheezes.

"Oh no!" I sob. So, it had been Eloise Platt drowning the baby after all.

My aunt recovers. "I had the presence of mind to pull Catherine's face into my coat so she wouldn't see it. But I started screaming, screaming at the top of my lungs. At that, Reginald came rushing out of the house in his shirt sleeves and dove into the water. He grabbed Eloise and... and the rest I don't know. I fainted."

I get up and put my hand on my aunt's protruding hip.

"I'm so sorry, Aunt Kittie, so very sorry."

But her voice is almost level when she adds, "that isn't all."

"What else?" My voice is a tiny squeak.

"I woke the next morning and saw Reginald sitting next to my bed with a look on his face I will never forget."

Aunt Kittie turns with difficulty on her back again and shoots me one of these glittering looks.

"The man was crying. I'd never seen Reginald cry before. He wept and wept. Despite my own distress and weakness, I asked him what ailed him.

'I've done something terrible, Katrina,' he sobbed. He always called me Katrina, never Kittie." Aunt Kittie sniffs as if the memory hurts her. "My head was swimming, but through the clouds I heard him say, 'I've drowned a dead baby.'" Aunt Kittie eyes me again, the light in her eyes shallower now and I feel myself shivering. Quite loudly, Aunt Kittie adds, "The Platt girl had twins, you see. The girl died at birth, but the boy survived. That's what Reginald told me, anyway."

"But why?" I hear myself ask, still shivering uncontrollably, "and what was Miss Platt doing in the lake? Was she trying to drown the other baby?"

"No. According to Reginald, she was delirious. She was only holding a blanket in her arms. She was... she was... trying to kill herself, though she may have thought she was holding the baby. Reginald said the boy was safely upstairs in the bedroom and that... that he'd called him Finley."

We both swallow and I grab my aunt's hand again. I feel bound to her in her sorrow.

"So why and how did Uncle Reginald "drown" the dead baby?" I hardly dare to ask about it.

"As I told you. He put it in the lake to wipe out any evidence of its existence. Put some heavy stones in a sack plus the poor dead infant and sunk the sack in the lake."

The eyes fire up again. "I'll never forgive him! And neither will the good Lord. A good man can turn bad,

Imogene Bowditch, and Reginald turned bad just to have an heir. He... he paid the London doctor so much money that the man emigrated to America so he would never open his mouth or put anything into writing. And then... then he had me locked up here because I was the only other person who knew the truth. He stole Catherine from me. Stole her from me as well. My baby, my baby!"

"Oh, Aunt Kittie!"

"There's always a catch in the perfect crime though, isn't there?" Suddenly her mischief is back, and I have a hard time switching with her fast change of mood.

"What do you mean, Aunt?"

"There is another witness."

"Who?"

"Richard Hopewell."

My mouth falls open. Is she talking of my landlord?

"Do you mean the Dartmond bookshop owner?"

"Oh, I don't know that," my aunt shrugs, "he was a young schoolboy in plus fours at the time."

"But how was he a witness? To what?"

"Reginald had taken the boy under his wings. He came from a poor family, eight kids or so. I guess Reginald was attracted to young boys, ugly as it may sound. Anyway, I was dragged down the stairs to the waiting ambulance, screaming at the top of my lungs all the terrible things Reginald had done. He'd brought our good name down and slung it through the mud, now hadn't he?" Aunt Kittie pauses, looks worried for a moment. "If Richard Hopewell is still alive, I'd like to apologise to him. He was only an innocent boy, but he bore witness to language he never should've heard. I remember him running from the house in his white shirt sleeves and brown trousers, though it was freezing. Running and running. I suppose back to Dartmond where he was from." She pauses again. "Strange how that image of the running boy is the most vivid one I have from that entire period. As if... as if... Richard was the only one who escaped our terrible fate."

I could see how tired Aunt Kittie was becoming. I actually felt drained myself. But I had one more question.

"Did you ever converse with Richard? I mean, did he speak?"

My aunt laughs again. "Converse isn't the right word, my dear. The boy spoke West Country slang as thick as butter on my Sunday toast."

"So you've been here at Ridgeview Asylum always, Aunt Kittie? You never even saw Finley?"

Silence. I want to caress her, to comfort her, but I don't know how.

"No. I never saw him. How is he?" The question is asked as if he *is* of some importance to her. Perhaps the hope he's a better squire than his father. Aunt Kittie must have been told her husband passed.

"He's fine, Aunt. Well, he's had a heart attack two months ago, and that's when the story of his adoption played up again, but he's fine now. I'm sure he'd love to come and visit you as well."

"Oh, there's no need for all that fuss, Imogene. Now get that doctor, will you?"

"I will, Aunt, and thank you so much. It makes sense that there were twins. I just never thought of that myself. I'll be back, Aunt. Soon, with Catherine! I promise."

"Get the doctor. Now!"

15

FITTING THE LAST PIECES OF THE PUZZLE

One month later

As you may have guessed, it took me considerable time to recover from my emotional visit to my aunt in the asylum. So many conflicting emotions there and a lot of guilt. I also miss my mother a great deal in this matter. I wish I could ask her why she, too, stopped visiting her favourite sister-in-law, in fact her only sister-in-law.

And what sort of relationship had my late Uncle Reginald with Aunt Kittie? How could he be so cruel to her? An heir to his estate at the expense of his wife. And what about my own positive memories of our summers there? They're all tarnished now.

Ah, this brain of mine. Sometimes I wish I could swap it for another one that doesn't flutter here and there like a flycatcher in a field. Next time I visit Aunt Kittie, I must ask for the Lady Pie recipe. Maybe it will help me, too, to calm my ruffled feathers.

Anyway, I moved heaven and earth to locate Aunt Kittie's daughter, Catherine, and then found out she returned to London last month and has been in the country since. I sent her this letter.

Dartmond, 4 October 1896

Dear Cousin Catherine,

I am glad to hear you are well and safe back in England and I hope you are in good health.

Much has happened since we last spoke with each other, which must be at least seven years. I was sorry to hear you couldn't come for your father's funeral.

Thank you again for your letter of condolence upon Thaddeus's passing. Your words were a most wondrous comfort to me.

I do hope you will come and visit the Cotswolds and us, now you're back in England. In fact, I have an urgent request for you on behalf of your mother.

I finally visited her in the asylum last week and found her quite well, but nearing the end of her earthly life. It is her express wish that I let you know she would very much like to see you before she is no longer with us. I would also very much like to see you again and am willing to accompany you to your mother's hospital, where she is taken excellent care of.

Pray tell me for how long you will be in England for and if such a visit could be arranged.

Your affectionate cousin,
Imogene Lynch-Bowditch

I HAVEN'T HEARD from Catherine since, but hope she'll come soon, and we can visit her mother together. Finley and Anna also got a brief note from me after much dilly dallying on my part.

Dartmond, 4 October 1896

Dear Finley and Anna,

I pray you are both in good health and spirit. I made a decidedly bold move and visited Lady Kittie Lowther in Ridgeview

Asylum after our mayor, Mr Banerjee, made an appointment for me through the asylum's head, Doctor Alardice, and the latter assured me there was no reason not to visit her.

Sparing you the details of the Lady's health at this moment, which is as good as can be expected for her age, I can tell you I was deeply moved by the visit. Especially what she told me she still remembered of that fateful Christmas in 1845.

According to Aunt Kittie, Miss Eloise Platt had two babies, one of which died at birth, the body of which was disposed of by Sir Reginald in Tiversack lake, and one babe survived-you, Finley-who was adopted as son and heir to Gladmers Manor. It looks like your mysterious adoption is solved and Miss Eloise Platt is your biological mother, after all.

Right now, I'm racking my old brain about how to get Miss Platt to tell us how she ended up at Gladmers pregnant.

Apologies for sharing this important information with you in a letter, but I thought you needed to know as soon as possible.

Hope to see you both soon.

Your affectionate cousin,
Imogene Lynch

AND THIS WAS the answer I got back.

Gladmers Manor, 9 October 1896

Dear Imogene,

Thank you for your letter, which we received in good order. We hope you are in good health as well.

Both Finley and I have great admiration for your forthrightness and tenacity in this case. We haven't said this before, but Thaddeus and you were the best detective pair the Cotswolds have ever seen, though we know you never considered yourself to be much involved in your husband's cases.

We were surprised at the news of your visit to Ridgeview Asylum, and we needed time to come to terms with the news of Finley's nearly confirmed birth mother. Still, we are grateful that–no matter the outcome–it has brought us all closer to a resolution.

If you could get Miss Platt to talk and she should confirm Lady Lowther's story, please let us know. We will consider what our next step is and let you know.

Finley asks if you think Lady Lowther would enjoy a visit from us? And we were also discussing Catherine, who is currently back in England. However, knowing you, you have already written to your cousin.

Next time we are in Dartmond, we will come to tea. And you know, the door is always open for you here. In the meantime, we wish you and Jasper all the best.

Be well, dear Imogene.

Your affectionate Anna and Finley

CLEARLY ANNA'S vision to write to me in this manner, but with Finley's agreement. I'm quite relieved they are taking the news of Miss Platt very likely being Finley's birth-mother so well. Also, that they're including Cousin Catherine in their thoughts. It would be good if this family grew a little closer.

I wonder, though, what Finley must think of his father. As far as I know, the two men were never very close, but it be hard to hear how your father obtained you in such a criminal matter. My own thoughts have turned quite sour when I think of my uncle's actions now, whereas the aunt I never knew seems to bring sunshine to my heart.

While I wait for Catherine's reaction, I go through all the details Aunt Kittie told me and my mind keeps circling to what she told me at the very end. Richard Hopewell witnessing the family drama and running away from it. Oh, it's such a gruesome image, it has even stuck in my mind though I never saw it.

"You tell me what to do about the landlord, Jasper dear," I say aloud, hoping my loyal dog will wake up and bring me some comfort. And the dear one does just that. He rises as stiffly as a frozen shadow and staggers towards me. With his snout on my feet, I caress his soft ears.

Meanwhile, I study Miss Platt's shop. I now understand she may truly believe she drowned that baby and lived with that secret all these years. There's no doubt Uncle Reginald silenced her as well, in some pressing manner.

That's another dilemma I face. How to tell her the truth? What does she remember from the day she delivered those babies at age sixteen? I feel so sorry for her.

But as if the times have already redeemed her, more customers seem to come and going steadily these days. Minnie Fritter just came out looking all smug with a parcel, and even Vicar Middlemiss went for a fitting of some sort yesterday.

Of course, I didn't see what he was fitted with, but was

told about the event by the baker's wife when I went for my yeast bread. She was all excited about it, as the Vicar had been Miss Platt's most fervent opponent.

I credit the change in tune to Mayor Banerjee. He's not just had a calming influence on me the two times I drank tea with him, but all the Dartmonders seem to unite around him and the community.

I haven't talked to Mr Banerjee about my visit to my aunt yet, but I will one of these days when I've designed a plan on how to make Miss Platt talk.

I have a guess, a wild guess, that my landlord Richard Hopewell's muteness is connected to this all. Didn't my aunt tell me he could talk as a boy? Oh, Jasper's ears are so velvety. I love caressing him this way and he doesn't protest, either.

Meanwhile, my thoughts drift back to what Mary Huckstep told me during the summer fair. I had walked over to her stall where she was selling pastries and cream puffs for the church bazaar. It must have been the sweet smell that wafted up Jasper's nose as he kept pulling his leash in Mrs Huckstep's direction.

"Ah, Mrs Lynch, the lady-with-the-small-appetite, as we call you. What can I do for you?" Her light-blue eyes had sparkled in the sun, and that's why I forgave her rather impertinent remark. Certainly, after she'd leaned in closer and whispered in my ear, "I heard you're a bit of an investigator, Mrs Lynch."

I raised my eyebrows. "Who told you that nonsense?"

"Ah Mrs Lynch, you will no longer tell me it's nonsense when I share something with you that might be of importance to your non-existent investigation."

"And what would that be, Mrs Huckstep?"

Jasper was meanwhile munching on one of the cream puffs and licked his lips in pure delight.

In her conspiratorial voice, the baker's wife continued, "My late father, bless his soul, was a classmate of Richard Hopewell at St Mary's Primary School in the 1840s." The blue eyes twinkle again to see if she has my attention. Well, she has.

"Go on," I urge her, as there are customers coming toward her stall.

"Your landlord wasn't born mute, Mrs Lynch. According to my father, Richard came back to school after the Christmas holidays in January 1846 and suddenly couldn't talk anymore. I thought this information might be helpful to you as Gertie told..." She clamps a hand over her mouth as she sees my gaze darken. My maid is talking. Now I will have to be stern with her, or she is out.

I had a stern talking-to with Gertie after Mrs Huckstep's revelation and the maid's promised never to give the townsfolk information about me again.

"They're so curious, Ma'am," she yammered, "they keep probing me with questions about you. I can't 'elp it."

I've become rather fond of my silly maid, and I guess she likes me too, so I just hope she sticks to her promise not to make me the subject of her conversations with other Dartmonders.

But anyway, I'm pondering what Mrs Huckstep told me about Richard Hopewell's sudden muteness in 1846. Combined with what my aunt told me about him talking West Country dialect. Richard Hopewell is my witness but not my most favourite person to interact with.

Would I have the audacity just to confront him with

my musings? It could go terribly wrong and make me the laughingstock for all that, if they get word of it through his wife.

Hmmm, let me think. I'm so tempted to go downstairs and just blow this thing wide open. Brooding over this matter for almost two years now isn't good for my heart. And even Finley has reconciled himself to probably being Miss Platt's son.

"Out with it, Jasper," I confide, getting up from my armchair while he also struggles to his feet. "You wait here for Neil while the mistress is going to do the most ridiculous thing she's ever done in her life. It's only a hunch, Jasper darling, only a hunch."

Without even putting on my coat, only my hat and gloves, I'm downstairs before I know it. Out of my front door and into the bookshop.

Thank God, there are no clients and both Hopewells are standing behind the counter wrapping books in gift paper.

I must look as if I've seen a ghost because Cornelia exclaims. "Everything all right, Mrs Lynch, no calamities, I hope?"

"Oh no, no," I assure her and then falter. I must explain why I've rushed into their shop like a madwoman.

"I just... I just wanted to ask you something."

But then I say nothing more so that they both stare at me. I fix my gaze on Mr Hopewell and he makes an impatient movement with his hand, indicating I should speak up or leave them in peace. I have no choice. I feel my cheeks go red and then my whole face grows hot right to the roots of my hair. *Oh Thaddeus*, I pray, *please help me.*

"Do you need a chair, Mrs Lynch?" Mrs Hopewell is already fetching a chair for me, and I sit down on it, strangely enough feeling close to crying. She puts a hand on my shoulder, a kind gesture I would not have expected from her.

"Is it something in your family, Mrs Lynch? Has something happened?"

And I nod. This is about my family, after all.

She sits down next to me while her husband continues to wrap the books.

"It can't be that bad that you can't tell us?" Her friendliness makes me even more vulnerable, as I've never seen the Hopewells as anything but cold and calculating. Maybe I have misjudged them, as I sometimes am too quick with my opinionated personality.

"It's about my cousin Finley," I begin and then the entire story follows up to and including what my aunt told me the week before.

While I tell the tale, Mr Hopewell's hands fall still. He's listening intently and then grabs a chair as well. When he becomes ashen grey, his face twitching and his hands shaking uncontrollably, I feel for him. He has had to live with his own nightmare all these years, unable to utter one word.

Sitting next to me, his wife observes him change as well.

"What is it, husband? Are you unwell?"

He starts howling like a thousand demons, wild and persistent with long-drawn shrieks, as if thrown into the recesses of hell. It hurts my ears. It's so sharp and agonizing. I see his wife run to him as he sinks onto his knees. The howling turns into uncontrolled sobbing, very unmanly but piercing the soul, nonetheless. I rise from my chair as well, not knowing what to do or how to comfort him.

"Fetch Doctor Suthmeer, please." Mrs Hopewell's dark-grey eyes plead with me, and I am already at the door when her husband wails, "Stop!"

"He is speaking!" His wife shrieks in bewilderment.

"Stop!" the bookshop owner shouts again. His sobbing subsides as he lies down on his shop floor, pale and aghast but not delirious anymore.

Together, we help him into a chair, and Mrs Hopewell quickly fetches him a glass of water from their kitchen at the back of the shop.

"There, there now," she repeats as if to a child. "Don't work yourself up, husband. I don't know what came over you."

"I..." he begins, and then again, "... I..." Nothing more. I don't think two people could hang more on the words of another human being than Mrs Hopewell and I at that moment.

"I've never heard him speak," she says in a trembling voice. "What in God's name has gone into him?"

"I..." he tries again, a voice deep from within his throat, "I... know... what the squire... did. Eloise... didn't drown the b... baby... It died, had he got rid of it... and he kept... he kept... the other one ... and... oh God... then he..t. locked up... the Lady." He swallows hard, takes a sip from his water while Mrs Hopewell's eyes become round in fear and astonishment. She seems to temporarily forget she's never heard his voice before.

"Husband, what are you talking about? What squire? What baby? What Lady?"

"There were t... two babies." He repeats.

I am not sure what to do, but interrupting him, I say in a soft voice, "Do you want me to tell what happened to you, Mr Hopewell, so you don't have to strain yourself?"

"N... no." Some of his former impatience surfaces. "I'll t... tell it. You w... weren't there."

"Let me get us some tea first. We're all so badly shaken," his wife suggests, but Mr Hopewell makes another impatient movement with his hand.

"S... sit quiet, wife. It's an e... effort as it is."

Mrs Hopewell and I sit quiet as church mice. The words come out of his mouth more fluently now, as if he needed to break free from a chain inside of him and is now liberated.

"I'd entered the hunting grounds of Gladmers Manor illegally because I'd found a field with snow geese. But the old squire caught me. He took me to the big house and said he'd punish me. I was so terrified. I'd taken my father's hunting rifle without him knowing it, so I was both trespassing and having to face the squire's and my father's wrath when I'd come home. But my mother had just given birth to my little sister. She was our tenth sibling, and my parents were very poor. My father... uh... wasn't a very good father. He preferred to spend the three shillings he earned in the freestone quarries in The Third Dagger Inn rather than giving it to my mother for food and clothes for us. Mother was still weak, and I wanted to surprise her by bringing home the spoils of my hunt. I couldn't wait to see all the faces of my sisters and brothers when my mother would cook the fat geese and we could finally fill our bellies to the brim. You see..."

He hesitates a moment, his face twisted in pain.

"Christmas Eve that year had meant rumbling stomachs for us. I'd felt so ashamed sitting in church hearing our empty bellies rumble when there was a pause in the singing. It just didn't feel good, and though I knew I was acting against the will of God, I hoped something good would come of it. Well, it didn't."

He pauses again, looking at his wife, who is gazing at him with her mouth open. As she's never heard his voice before, she doesn't seem able to grasp it. We sit and wait for the rest of the story, most of which was already told to me by my aunt. But hearing Richard explain it himself is heart-breaking.

"The old squire was... uh... had a fondness for boys. But I didn't know that when he took me home and spoiled me with cakes and lemonade. I first thought I'd landed in Heaven, such a grand house and all that food. Though I felt bad not being able to share the delicacies with my brothers and sisters and, of course, with my weak mother. But then he made me stay in his bedroom and... and I was really afraid because my parents didn't know where I was and... it wasn't pleasant what he... uh ... the squire did to me, touching me ... It was awful." Richard squeezes his eyes together in agony at the memory. Cornelia takes her husband's hand, while her own face shows utter shock. She clearly feels she knows nothing of her husband's past. I feel myself swallow, forbidding my mind from imagining the awful scene.

Richard looks as if he can't get any air, pulls wildly at the collar of his shirt until the button comes off.

"The squire sent me home with his coach later that evening and the coach dropped me off at the edge of Dartmond. But he'd said I had to come back every

Saturday for my punishment, or he would tell the constable." Richard looks helplessly at his wife. "There were strange things going on in that house. It was haunted. A baby cried all the time, and the mistress howled like a pack of dogs. And then that horrible squire with his groping hands. I thought I was going mad, but I hadn't seen the worst yet." He stops, wipes the sweat from his forehead.

"There was suddenly a lot of commotion, and I saw the Lady being dragged down the stairs in a nightdress by two men in long, white coats. She was screaming at the top of her lungs while she was pushed into an ambulance. "I'm not mad. You are mad! You've stolen a child. Finley isn't your child. It's Eloise Platt's child. She had two babies, two babies! And I know you threw the dead one in the lake. You told me so yourself! You're a murderer and a child thief. And abusing that poor boy over there! You're mad yourself, Reginald Lowther."

Richard looks from his wife to me, his face stricken and pale as an old lamp. "It all made little sense to me, but the words clung to me like ivy. I started running. Somehow, I kept running, blind and mute. I didn't stop until I was home. My clothes were torn, I was wild with madness. My father, drunk as always, spanked me hard and sent me to the coal shed for a day and a night. I don't know how I survived, but I did."

Richard slowly rises from his chair and stands on stiff legs before his wife, looking down at her with so much love in his eyes. I feel my heart fill up. Putting a hand on her shoulder, he gives it a little squeeze.

"I've been miserable every day of my life, until I met you, my dear Cornelia. You gave me some sunshine again and here we are now. Back in the past, that horrible past. No wonder Eloise Platt never talked about what she went through. And I couldn't even if I had wanted to tell you. Not for the life of me. Until now."

I have to disclose information my aunt told me that Richard doesn't seem to know.

"So, you never saw Eloise Platt at Gladmers Manor? Or saw her walk into the lake with a blanket? You only heard a baby cry inside the house?"

"That's correct. It was from the Lady's words that I understood Eloise, whom I knew, of course, and knew she'd been missing, had her babies at Gladmers Manor. I ... I just evaded her all my life."

"But you can confirm she never killed her child. That it was Sir Reginald who callously disposed of an already dead baby?"

"Only from hearsay." Richard is keenly aware I'm the constable's wife now, though I mess with my interrogation by putting the words into his mouth. I'm so confused myself.

"I wonder why Eloise said she did it?" Cornelia chimes in rather timidly.

I hesitate, then say what I think. "She probably believes she was holding a baby in that blanket. That's why her subconsciousness told her to confess when the Fritters' boys came home with the skull."

"What a terrible business! We have to help her." Richard seems to have found his strength again.

"We must have a cup of tea first," Cornelia decides, "just to get some warmth in us."

"Yes, yes, of course, wife. Tea is what we need."

While his wife is tottering in the kitchen, Richard

Hopewell says to me, "I wonder how to approach, Eloise. I feel so bad for having known her tragedy all those years and being unable to do anything about it. I was the only one who knew, the helpless one."

"That's not true, Mr Hopewell. I got the information from Lady Kittie Lowther. She knows as well."

He nods. "Yes, she does."

He looks stricken again. "I could... I should have written it down, but I was so afraid of Sir Reginald Lowther's power. So, I just stuck my head in the sand and pretended to also have a grudge against Eloise. I'm a bad person."

"No, you're not a bad person, Mr Hopewell. You couldn't have acted other than you did. And what matters is that we can amend our actions."

He looks straight at me. "Eloise Platt *has to* be told the truth, not just for her own sake, but for everyone's sake. What happened that made her so desperate she wanted to drown herself, thinking she was taking her own child with her, maybe even both."

I agree with my landlord. No mother in her right mind would do such a thing.

"There must be a terrible tragedy behind it, and that's why we have to approach her with great care and sensitivity."

"We?" Richard looks at me in dismay.

"Yes, we, Mr Hopewell. You and I. After all, there's something for her to gain in it. She has a son, and he's doing well. It may be a slight comfort to her in her old age."

He nods slowly. "The poor girl has suffered enough, carrying that terrible secret with her for her entire life.

She isn't a bad person. Never was. Always ready to help others. It's just so strange that in a tight community as Dartmond, we never suspected there was such a black chapter in her past."

"And we would never have known if Sir Reginald hadn't confessed the adoption on his deathbed," I add.

Mrs Hopewell comes back with the tea. The full and brisk taste of the Ceylon tea, with its notes of citrus, chocolate, and spice, perks us all up.

"Are you ready for a visit to your neighbour across the street tomorrow morning, Mr Hopewell?" I ask as I rise from my chair to bid them farewell. The last hour has brought us so much closer.

"I am, Mrs Lynch. And I thank you sincerely for giving me back my voice. You're truly a wonderful pursuer of righteousness and truth."

"Thank you." My voice quivers. His genuine praise means everything to me.

"And please call us Richard and Cornelia."

"Then you must call me Imogene."

"Imogene, my saviour, it is!"

16

WHEN THE TRUTH IS THE WORST

It seems almost unnecessary to tell you I didn't sleep a wink last night. This predicament with Miss Platt is affecting my health. It needs to find closure one way or the other, or I fear I'll catch a disease over it.

Tossing and turning in my linen bedding all night, I've also upset Jasper's nightly rest. So now, I'm up at the crack of dawn, washing and dressing elegantly but simply. My sage-green bombazine dress will do just fine for the occasion.

I'm on my way to the kitchen before Gertie wakes up to make me a cup of tea. Darjeeling it will be, as it reminds me of its soothing effect on my frayed nerves when I visited the mayor.

So here am I now, looking around my scant, rented kitchen, wondering what to do with my life. Jasper has waddled to my side, still half asleep but wagging his tail in hopes of yesterday's pork sausage.

As I feed him and wait for the kettle to boil, I stare at the row of gleaming copper pans on the rack above the sink as if they have an answer for me. And then, at that very minute, I stop my thoughts, that nagging feeling that's been with me since Thaddeus passed.

"Enough is enough!" I say out loud. Jasper looks up, still licking his lips, with a surprised look in his brown eyes as if saying, "What's the mistress up to now?"

Walking with my teacup back to the sitting room, Jasper right behind me, I make a firm decision. I've uncovered the truth. Richard and I are going to confront Miss Platt. That's it. That's all. More I cannot and will not do. If she refuses to answer our questions, I'm done with this case.

It's solved, my dear benedict, whether it comes out in the open. Of course, it would be best if she acknowledged the truth so it can be forgiven and forgotten, but if that is not happening, I'll go no further than this. This is my ultimate word on it.

A great sense of relief settles over my heart, as if a heavy stamp that was pressing on my chest is removed. It might be the Darjeeling; more likely it's my resolution. I'll face Miss Platt calmly. Leave it up to her.

TWO HOURS LATER, I still feel almost light-hearted as I descend the stairs and enter the Hopewells' shop. For a moment, I wonder if yesterday was a figment of my imagination and my landlord never uttered a word, but he greets me with a chirpy, "Good morning, Imogene. Beautiful day, isn't it?" I'm glad it wasn't my lack of night rest that played tricks with me.

"It is, Richard." And not able to curb my curiosity, I

ask, "How have customers reacted to your sudden oral skills?"

His wife, who has come to his side, smiling at me, answers, "Oh, I have been doing the talking as the early risers came for their newspapers. We didn't want any strange faces before you've been to visit Miss Platt."

I nod. That's a wise decision. Her blue bicycle is parked against her shop, so she has arrived as usual.

"Shall we cut to the chase?" Richard asks. "Wife, you come with me, in case my voice breaks."

The three of us cross the street and I feel multiple Dartmond eyes on us, though none knows what this is about. From the moment we enter Miss Platt's shop, I feel she's on the defence. My earlier encounters with her have made me understand she is an intelligent person, so she already knows what this is about, only not that it will come from Richard Hopewell.

"Good day, Miss Platt." I am the first to speak. She pretends to be busy winding Brussels lace on a spool and just nods to us. We are lucky there are no other customers in her shop.

Richard clears his throat, which makes her look up in wonderment.

"Eloise," he begins and then falters, "I... I assume it's s... still all right to call you by your Christian name?"

"Heavens, Richard." She backs away from her counter as if wanting to disappear into the wall behind her. The lace spool tumbles to the floor. "Since when can you talk again?" The grey eyes behind the round spectacles become large with fear. Her hands claw at the wall as if to support herself.

"Please, Eloise, don't be afraid," the bookseller pleads.

"I haven't come to do you harm, and neither have Cornelia nor Imogene."

"Why are you here, then?" Miss Platt says shrilly, almost in a child's voice. We stay behind Richard's back as he takes a step in poor Eloise's direction.

"Do you think we can sit down for a moment? Close your shop for the time being?"

"But why, Richard? What's going on?" I see her desperately seeking for a way out of what she knows is to come.

In the mellowest tone I've ever heard a man speak, he answers, "But you know, Eloise. It is time. Really time."

As if magnetized by that gentle voice, she walks to her shop door like an automaton and turns the key in the lock. When she faces us again, there are tears in her eyes that mist up her spectacles. My heart mourns for her, but there is little I can do now.

Unsteady on her feet, she wildly grabs objects in her path to stay balanced, knocking over a tailor's dummy and an ornamental Delft blue vase that shatters in a thousand pieces. Richard hastens towards her and escorts her by her elbow to a chair.

"We'll clear that in a minute. Let me get you a glass of water." Cornelia already takes the liberty of entering Miss Platt's kitchen at the back of her shop.

Of course, these people have known each other since they were children and know what to do. I slip into a chair, unable to face Miss Platt's agony. She is whimpering. I can't endure it any longer.

"I am so sorry, Miss Platt. It's all my fault. All my probing. I am sorry. Please forgive me. I never intended to burden you with so much distress."

Cornelia passes around glasses of water and a hand-kerchief for Eloise. It is silent for a while except for her sniffling. Then she says in an almost normal voice,

"I don't blame you, Mrs Lynch. I know you only want clarity for your family. I would want the same."

"Even if the price is this high?" I need to ask.

"Yes."

Then she turns to Richard. In only a whisper, she puts forth, "I took you down with me, Richard. Sir Reginald told me to shut up, or he'd know where to find both of us. It was also you I suffered for all these years. But there was never a way to tell you. He would have killed me. So, I stayed quiet after I came back, just like you."

Richard puts an arm on her sleeve. "We've both suffered enough, Eloise."

She nods and then directs her eyes to me. They are still wet with tears, but she controls herself now. "And your Aunt Kittie and Cousin Catherine. They were victims of him as well. I did see them, and I heard your aunt scream in the house. It's no wonder Catherine didn't come to Sir Reginald's funeral. He was... he was a monster."

Richard nods, and I feel those same shivers again for a secret I never knew.

"My Aunt Kittie remembers it all," I inform Miss Platt. "That's how I knew. I visited her last week."

Eloise is silent for a while, digesting this new information, clearly going back to her own memories of living at Gladmers Manor, which I now understand must have been hell, even apart from her unwanted pregnancy.

In her resolute voice, she announces, "I'll tell the entire story to you. But I cannot face telling it twice. I think we need an official to be a witness as well. I don't particularly like Constable Walsh, but maybe Mr Banerjee or Constable Candy from Landdulton?"

I admire her pluck and her insight.

"And what about the press?" I ask.

"You can talk to Miss Philpot. I trust you'll tell the truth."

"I'll see if Mr Banerjee has time right now." Richard gets up from his chair.

"I'd prefer to stay in my shop." Miss Platt has sufficiently recovered to make her own decisions.

"I'll be back in two seconds." The bookseller is already out of the door, clearly forgetting that his voice will be a big surprise to our mayor.

WHEN RICHARD RETURNS with Mr Banerjee on his heels, we have already prepared coffee for the gentlemen and tea for the ladies. Miss Platt is sitting in the most comfortable chair in her shop, used for ladies visiting when their husbands need a fitting. I have pulled the shades for the windows so no nosy Dartmonders can peer in. The gas lamps are lit and there is a fire in the fireplace.

We all sit and wait until Miss Platt is ready.

"I'll try to tell it as short as I can because that way it will hurt less," she begins. "I was on my way to Gladmers Manor in mid-April 1845 to deliver a parcel from our shop. I was sixteen. I knew the way but took a shortcut through Hungry Summit Hills because there were heavy rain clouds in the sky, and it was a long walk."

She pauses, takes a deep breath. "I was attacked,

suddenly, from the back and grabbed. I was terrified because I knew the stories of what had happened to other girls who met the vagrant. I don't want to tell what he did to me. I only know that when he left, I lay as if I was dead and waited for a very long time until I was sure he was gone. I needed to wash myself, which I did in a small pool nearby. My clothes were ruined, and I was bruised and scratched.

"I didn't go to Gladmers Manor but went home. I don't know how I got home, but my parents were still in the shop, and I crept upstairs and threw the clothes away and put on new clothes. My sister Beatrice was living next door. She was just married and pregnant with her first child."

A pin could drop. It is that silent. It seems as if nobody is even breathing.

"My parents asked what had happened to me and I said I had fallen and bruised myself. That was the end of it. But during the summer, my tummy began to grow, and I looked exactly as Beatrice had done before she had her child. I wasn't stupid. I knew what had happened to me, but I was in a complete panic. My parents had noticed nothing yet. Then I remembered that there was talk of Mildred Godkim, Farmer Godkim's daughter who'd been sent to a place for unwed mothers in Bristol. I was so desperate."

Eloise looks at us, momentarily stuffing the crumpled handkerchief in her mouth, but then she straightens her shoulders and continues, "I went to the farm and asked her mother. She was kind, I knew she was, and she helped me. She gave me the coach fare to Bristol. But then... then... we had an accident. I knew the driver was drunk when I boarded, but what choice had I? It was horrible. We fell and fell and then the coach was upside down in the ravine.

"I lost consciousness. I don't know for how long, but when I woke up, it was pitch-black. I could see the stars way above me. It was cold as well, cold as ice. Sometime in October. I heard nothing, just the wind flapping the curtains of the coach. There had been three other people traveling with me, but I didn't know who they were or where they were after the crash."

She pauses again, taking off the misted-up spectacles and dabbing her eyes. I feel like someone has punched a hole in my stomach and all my life-force is seeping out. Pregnant after being abused, on the run from her family, and then ending up in an accident of which we all now know only she survived.

Her voice starts again, almost emotionless now.

"I recall little of the next days. I managed to clamber up from Lockedows ravine and seek shelter in some sort of cave. I just lay there, waiting for death. Welcoming it."

Miss Platt's eyes briefly flutter to mine, as if asking forgiveness, but I understand her so well. What would I have done in her situation? Exactly the same. Sometimes death seems the only answer.

"Then, one day, I don't know if it was morn or afternoon, but it was light... I felt something pushing in my side. It was very faint; I was almost gone, but then I heard a voice. It was a male voice. I didn't care at that moment anymore whether it was good or bad folk. Dogs were barking as well, and I understood it had been the snout of a dog in my side. The days after that incident are foggy in my memory."

Mr Banerjee is sitting on a straight chair across from me, still as a Roman statue, his eyelids half closed over his eyes, but I know he's listening intently. Only the deep lines that mark his otherwise smooth forehead show how distressed he also is.

"Next thing I know," Miss Platt proceeds with her monologue, "is that I'm lying in the softest bed I've ever lain in. Everything is white and silent, so I assume I'm in heaven. I hear voices in the room, but they're all very natural and go in one ear and out the other.

"So, I'm really surprised when I see an old man's face with a lorgnette bent over me, asking me how I'm feeling. This wasn't how I had pictured our Lord and Saviour, but I remember thinking to myself: what do I know of Heaven? I wasn't expecting to be granted access after my behaviour."

Despite herself, the shadow of a smile glides over her sorrowful face. This must have been for her the only positive in a long and awful journey.

"When I gained a little more strength, Sir Reginald Lowther came into my room and made a proposal to me." A deep sigh. "The proposal you all now know." Her hands go helplessly into the air. "What could I do? I was in no position to do anything, and it seemed plausible, logical, feasible." Another pause. "It was just that, of course, that could have solved everybody's problems, but I wrecked it."

The next pause is even longer. I fear she won't go any further, will not reveal how she came to that unimaginable decision to drown herself when she was given a ticket out of it. Everyone sits frozen and frightened, but Miss Platt is strong, stronger than she knows herself.

"The babies were born on Christmas Day. A girl and a boy. I remember little of the birth, but the London doctor, the one with the lorgnette, and a nurse were there. I was in a total panic, not understanding what my body was doing and why. The pains were..." Strangely enough, she smiles again. "Well, every woman knows what birth pains are like."

As both Cornelia and I are childless, though I had my miscarriages, it seems an odd saying, but I know what she means.

"I couldn't rest after the babies were born and asleep in the room with me. Not even after the doctor had given me some sort of sedation. I couldn't. My mind wouldn't let go. I was going to be found out."

She takes off her spectacles to dab her eyes. "Then the doctor told me the girl was dead and I remember thinking, there you go, you're doomed, Eloise Platt. I knew Sir Reginald only wanted the boy, but for me, it was done. I got up. I don't know how, grabbed my little girl's blanket, and walked out of the house, not feeling the cold, the pain, the agony anymore. I was free. I was free to die..."

She stops, dry-eyed, still white, then adds in the most death-like voice, "It wasn't to be."

"Why do you think Sir Reginald didn't simply let you die?" I have to ask this hard question. It would have solved a problem for him, after all.

Her grey eyes lit up. "Fie, he might drown a small infant, but getting rid of a grown girl is quite another matter." She blinks, "At least I think that was his reason for rescuing me."

There is another terrible question that my constable-like mind can't help putting forward.

"Did you ever see if the little girl was really dead?"

She nods but doesn't speak.

"Did Sir Reginald tell you what he planned to do with the body?"

"No, but I understood when her... little head was found."

Tears fill her eyes again.

"Enough questions, Mrs Lynch." Mr Banerjee's voice is kind but resolute, and I hold my tongue.

The mayor takes up his leader's role by declaring, "I'm incredibly proud of you all and humbled to be part of such a breakthrough revelation. But we will call it a day for now and take the day off to recuperate. If any of you need mental or other assistance, I'm at your disposal all day. So please just let Hardy know and I'll come straight away." He gets up, straightens his coat, and bows reverently to the four of us.

We stay together in Eloise's shop for the rest of the day. Talking, some crying, and finally eating a simple tea, as four friends who've gone through an ordeal together would do.

FINALLY A MERRY CHRISTMAS IN DARTMOND

25 December 1896

Oh, I wish my Thaddeus was here on this glorious Christmas Day! My fifty-first birthday! His absence is the only sadness I know. I'm sitting here at my window with Jasper at my feet, looking down into a very merry Darren Street. Miss Platt has chaired the Dartmond Christmas Decoration Committee once more this year, and it shows. There is no one that does the job better than our former 'mayor.'

The decorations are a pure delight — gas lanterns that flicker in the slowly falling snowflakes, amidst strings of fresh-cut evergreen trees with beads, tinsel, ornaments, and jewelled baubles. Mayor Banerjee told her not to spare any expense this year.

My house smells delightful, of spicy tea, mince pies and Christmas cake, but Gertie has also put two scented candles with cinnamon and cardamom on the mantlepiece that fills the room with a special aroma.

And then there's my teeny-weeny spruce tree that gives off that wonderful woody, piney scent mixed with a citrusy odour. As I'm a scent-oriented creature, as you must have realized by now, Christmas has always been my favourite time of year. Except for last year, but that was an exception.

I'm comfortable in my chair, having just returned from Mass at Trinity Church and being congratulated on my birthday by everyone. Even Vicar Middlemiss seems to grasp Dartmond's revival and lectured from the pulpit as if inspired by a flash of lightning. I should, of course, say 'inspired by the Holy Spirit,' but I'm still not convinced that's the case with our vicar. Though he tries as best as he can.

There's Mrs Winnifred Herriot on her husband's arm, parading through our main street. Such a pretty pair and so exquisitely dressed. I'll say no more for fear you'll find my tongue too sharp. Mrs Huckstep told me they're off to Cairo in the new year, doing a cruise down the Nile. Ah well, some folks blow the loud horn plenty out there.

Which brings me to Cousin Catherine. She's on her way here, should arrive any time now. Of course, my apartment is too cramped to lodge her here, so she'll stay at Gladmers Manor. That's where she'll go first, and then Anna and Finley will accompany her, and we'll all have tea here. Celebrate both our birthdays like we did in the old days.

Then we're off to the grand Christmas dinner in the town hall. Mr Banerjee insisted we'd celebrate Christmas together as a community, and everyone agreed.

When I told him I had guests, he said with his usual

generosity, "bring them, Mrs Lynch. They will be our guests of honour."

I'm just doubting about Jasper but as he likes company so much, I think I'll tug him along. It would be so sad to leave him here on his own, and Neil is escorting Gertie anyway so he can carry him down.

We're all set. I can't wait. I'm wearing my burgundy-red silk dress with the French sleeves and embroidery down the front. The skirt is partly of a slightly darker, soft velvet and the neckline and sleeves have my favourite Cluny lace. Two ribbons accentuate the waistline.

I know this dress suits my complexion and figure, but I was in doubt whether to wear it. Thaddeus adored this dress, so it makes me remember the times I wore it in his presence.

But then I said to myself, "Imogene, dear girl, you've done a good job and he would want you to round it off in this dress." That's why I'm sitting in it now and don't feel sad but, in my own little way, quite accomplished.

TOWARDS THE END of the afternoon, when the dusk is already upon us, we enter the town hall. Cousin Catherine's arm through mine–she doesn't depart from my side for one second–I don't believe my eyes. The young people have decorated the renaissance hall with all the Christmas paraphernalia you can imagine, and there's even a string quartet playing Christmas carols in the corner. An enormous table with white tablecloths has been set up in the middle of the room, decked with winter floral arrangements, candles and a variety of plates and cutlery.

Cousin Catherine, who's exactly the same size as me and as willowy, squeezes my arm.

"Oh, it's so good to be back in rural England. How I've missed this cosy sociability. Cairo is all about standing and who knows who, you see." I wouldn't know, but I believe her. I'm just so happy to have her close again, and Anna and Finley. My family. Jasper, who's trotting up front, wags his tail as if he's the guest of honour.

Mr Banerjee, clad in a forest-green, long-cut coat and black trousers, his hair pomaded and the tips of his long moustache shiny with wax, makes his way around the table towards us, his brown eyes shining and his hands stretched out.

"There you are! My guests of honour. Happy birthday, Mrs Lynch, and happy birthday, Sir Lowther. I'm so glad to finally welcome you, Sir and Ladies Lowther. May I compliment you all on your fine appearance?"

He shakes hands with as all and accompanies us to the head of the table, that to my embarrassment is laden with wrapped parcels in all sorts and sizes. Dartmond hasn't forgotten my birthday, nor that of the secret Christmas Baby.

After us, the rest of the community is trickling in. I see one familiar face after the other. Mr Banerjee insists on me sitting at the head of the table, which makes me quite self-conscious, but he assures me.

"You are really our most important guest, Mrs Lynch. You've brought this town together like no one has done before you. We celebrate your great work, which started with your late husband."

Oh, I feel my cheeks go red with the praise. Heavens, I don't deserve it, but Jasper seems to disagree and utters his rare "woof."

As I'm seated like Queen Victoria herself, flanked by my cousins and sister-in-law, pretty Claudia Pinkerton, the daughter of the inn owner, comes to fill our glasses with sweet-scented sherry. For once, I decide I'll drink the alcoholic beverage, as it might calm my nerves.

"It's quite something, isn't it?" Finley says on my right, and I know he, too, understands this is a major change in our family dynamics. I nod and sip my sherry that instantly goes to my head.

Catherine puts a hand on my arm and whispers in my ear. "I honestly would never have thought Dartmond would accept a mayor like Mr Banerjee. How rapidly society is changing, and for the better." I nod again, feeling as if I've lost my tongue, glad Jasper's warm snout is on my foot and the band is not out of tune.

Timothy waves at me as he enters the hall in between his parents, his light hair combed deftly over his head, proudly erect in his best blue suit. Mrs Pocock smiles friendly at me, but her husband, whom I haven't yet met, is more focused on talking with Vicar Middlemiss.

The shopkeepers throng in together, the Hucksteps with daughter Lucy, the Fritters only with young Alfie, as Neil is standing in the corner with Gertie. Grocer Herby shuffles in with his rather introverted wife Francis, then there's Butcher Wilson with son Gerald. The Hopewells come in last and are directed to places near us. I'm glad to see them. We've become so much closer these days.

Then there's Miss Hermine Tow in an extravagant strawberry-pink dress, but I have to hand it to her. If there's one person who can pull this off, it's Hermine. She just loves it, how all eyes turn to her, even those of the mayor.

Dr Suthmeer, looking old and unsure of himself, comes in with his bustling wife. Then Undertaker Crowle rubbing his hands in glee with a sour-looking Icie Crowle at his side. Hardy Crowle was already helping the mayor with all the preparations.

Coach driver Cadden comes in, turning his cap between his fingers and slipping into his place without a word and without looking at anyone.

More marching than walking, here comes Constable Columbus Walsh, with–to my surprise–Young Axel at his side. Oh, it is so good to see my young friend in his deft uniform. Axel leaves the older policeman's company and comes to shake my hand.

"Well done, Mrs Lynch, and happy birthday! I always knew you were as good and as tenacious as your husband."

I colour again. "I don't know about that, Axel, but your compliment is wonderful. I'm so glad to see you."

"Yes, it was very kind of Mr Banerjee to invite me. I couldn't say no, though my parents found it strange that I wasn't having Christmas dinner with them. I told them next year would be soon enough."

"I'll talk to you later," I say, as my eyes feast on all the people in their Sunday best and with smiles on their faces. I just wonder where Miss Eloise Platt is, but while I wonder, I have another surprise. Theresa Philpot, dressed in something that looks more like a man's trousers than a skirt, bearing her white teeth as she strides in and shakes my hand vigorously.

"Here for work, Mrs Lynch. Can I have an interview with you later?"

"Heavens," I say, taking a quick nip from my sherry, and then again. "Heavens, I guess so."

The only people missing are the Herriots and Miss Platt.

"Any idea if the Herriots are coming?" I ask Cornelia.

"I heard they weren't. They have guests at the big house, but to be honest, I think they consider this town hall dinner beneath them."

Just what I thought. They will fit in perfectly in Cairo if I am to believe my cousin.

"What about Eloise?" I ask my landlady again.

"Oh, she'll come, don't worry."

I see Mr Banerjee almost waltz to the door and in comes Miss Eloise Platt, on the mayor's arm. She looks festive in a brand-new, checked dress of her own making, lovely purples and greens with great lace finishing touches, her spectacles clean and her grey hair done up nicely. Erect and smiling, she walks to the other head of the table, where she takes a seat next to Mr Banerjee. Smiling, she waves a hand at us, and we wave back, raising our glasses at the same time.

Now all Dartmond is together.

But just as the mayor taps his glass for silence to deliver his speech, the door opens again and, in a wheel-chair, wrapped warmly in woollen blankets, her glasses askew, pushed in my Nurse Grain, is Aunt Kittie Lowther with a freshly baked Lady Pie in her lap.

We all stand, we all clap, and she bows to us rever-ently. Catherine and Finley hasten to her side.

Oh, it's a sight for sore eyes and I think my heart will

burst with happiness. Thank you, Thaddeus, for burdening me with your brown file.

It is closed for good.

I take a sizable bite of the Lady Pie. Oh, it tastes as sweet and flavourful as first love. I can tell you Jasper isn't getting any of this. This time it's for me.

MERRY CHRISTMAS, everyone!

DID YOU ENJOY Imogene's attempt at being a first-time amateur sleuth?

Find out what happens when she travels to Cairo with Cousin Catherine. Preorder The Peculiar Vanishing Act of Mr Ralph Herriot. And read Chapter 1 if you click through!

WANT TO READ more Mrs Lynch stories now? Join my Newsletter and get The Disappearance of Miss Phoebe Hewlett for free.

1

TASTER: THE PECULIAR VANISHING ACT OF MR RALPH HERRIOT

CHAPTER 1 CATHERINE'S MOST PREPOSTEROUS PROPOSAL

Honeydew Mansion, April 1896

I have everything in the world a person needs: good health, a lovely home, a doting dog, family who care for me, and more than enough worldly goods to satisfy even a hungry soul. Yet, I'm as melancholy as an Irish melody.

I returned home to my lovely house just outside Landdulton in early February 1896 and the first weeks were heaven. You'd think I missed my cramped apartment on Darren Street in Dartmond, watching the Dartmonders go from bakery to butcher and back, but I did not. Not one second.

Roly-poly Jasper has settled back in at home like he's never been away. Oh, I think fondly of my maid Gertie and her beau Neil Fritter. And young Timothy Pocock, of course, has captured a place in my heart for good. Even my landlords, the Hopewells, despite our early squabbles, became quite good friends. My thoughts also frequently return to the languid Miss Platt and our colourful mayor, Mr Rahul Banerjee.

But all of them are not as much missed as I had missed my home.

Or at least what I thought was home. With Mrs Peaton singing in the kitchen and Jasper running around Tiversack Lake as a young puppy, life seemed to laugh at me again. Tat dragging case of the secret Christmas baby finally solved. My conscience was clear.

Having fulfilled my Thaddeus's last request, I knew it was the right thing to leave my Dartmond friends behind and return to my spacious, sun-filled villa with my own furniture and lovely garden.

Another recent delight was Cousin Catherine's stay with me at Honeydew Mansion for two weeks. It was sheer heaven. We'd both forgotten how we used to dote on each other as children and though we'd missed most of each other's adult years, it was as if time had stood still for us. I was so sad when she left, but understood she had other obligations.

"Dearest Imogene, my brother will think we've fallen out with each other when I'm not at least spending some time at home with him and Anna at Gladmers. But do come and stay with me in London in the spring. Or even accompany me to Egypt when I return there in May."

She'd laughed that captivating, tinkling laugh of hers, a sound that cannot help but make you smile as well, full of mirth and mischief

"London I could consider, but that camel-smelling, desert country is not for me," I had retorted.

"Oh, you're wrong there, dear cousin, Egypt smells

wonderful." Catherine had stretched her long fingers one by one into the air.

"Cinnamon, frankincense, lemongrass, myrrh, rose. These scents far overpower the murky camel smell. Do come with me to Shepheard's Hotel in Cairo and drown yourself in oriental scents and colours. Amazing company there as well. It'll do you so much good!"

Why does this conversation flood into my mind right now? Who talks of Egypt? What nonsense. Only world travellers and sweet eccentrics like Catherine traipse to these dangerous countries. Also, I have Jasper to consider. I can take the darling with me to London but not to Cairo.

Talking of Jasper, it is time for his walk. Oh, I simply must force myself to get up from this chair and move my old bones. This house is so full of Thaddeus still. Every ornament, his chair, even his reading glasses are still on the glass-topped table next to his chair. It's just that *The Cotswolds Times* isn't folded underneath his glasses anymore.

THE SILENCE, his silence, his absence.

I FEEL as empty as a bird's nest in December, now Catherine's invigorating presence has left me. Some people are like a lamp lit in a darkened room. Catherine is like that, and I'm the moth fluttering to the light though I don't particularly like this comparison.

Without further ado, I drag my feet to the kitchen, where the delicious smell of freshly baked bread wafts into my nose. Jasper rushes ahead to push his nose against the kitchen door with a wildly wagging tail.

Mrs Peaton is singing Verdi's *Anvil Chorus* in her clear libretto. I pause to listen for a moment.

See how the clouds melt away
from the face of the sky when the sun shines, its brightness
beaming;
just as a widow, discarding her black robes,
shows all her beauty in brilliance gleaming.

THE SONG and her voice move me. I know she's not singing about me, but it feels that way. I may have discarded my black robes, but my soul is still full of mourning. That has nothing to do with the clothes one wears.

"Good morning, Mrs Peaton."

She stops singing, a smile on her round face, her arms to her elbows covered in flour.

"Ah, Mrs Lynch. Good to see you up. I need your advice on..." She stops, her kneading hands fall silent. "What is it, Mrs Lynch? You look unwell."

I sink down on a kitchen chair, sighing. It is no use pretending I'm all chirpy when I'm not. Jasper seems to pick up on my mood, his tail falls silent. Droopy brown eyes investigate my face. These two creatures depend on me. I must make an effort to feel better.

"I'm alright, Mrs Peaton." The lie comes out falteringly. "What was it you wanted to consult me on?"

She wipes the flour from her hands and then comes over to the sink to wash them.

"We're going to have a cuppa." Is her short reply.

"How have you managed here on your own, Mrs Peaton?" I ask her back, a question that was long overdue ,but it's the first time we're actually alone in the house since my return from Dartmond.

Busy with putting the kettle on and getting the teacups out she doesn't immediately answer me then looks straight at me with those clear blue eyes.

"It has been good and not so good, to tell the truth. The good thing is that I love this house and as it's big and laborious, it's kept me busy. But it's been darn silent. I'm glad you're back, Mrs Lynch."

"Even when I'm not really good company?" I pull a face.

"Oh, but when Lady Lowther was here, you were perfect company, and it was so wonderful to cook for people besides myself again." My housekeeper looks at me with these knowing eyes. You cannot be in someone service for over twenty-five years and not know them intimately. I know she doted on Thaddeus as well.

"Why don't you go and visit London this spring, Mrs Lynch?"

I shake my head.

"I can't, Mrs Peaton and you know why. It's not proper to hop from one place to the other like a restless robin. I have to get accustomed to being here on my own. And there are so many of Mr Lynch's things that I have to clear out, like his desk and his wardro..." She raises a pudgy hand.

"Stop right there, Ma'am. Nobody says you have to do these things right now. I'm dusting the constable's office every week and I air his clothes so there will be no moths in them."

"But..."

"But you'd rather be miserable?" She interrupts me, "Grieving one's husband takes years. and I was only married to Mr Peaton for five years when he was killed in the Crimean war. Yet I was so grateful that you took me in, and I didn't have to stay in our silent marital home any longer. I think it is the same for you, Mrs Lynch. You'll feel better when you're away. In time it will be easier and easier to come here."

"But what about you? I can't leave you on your own again?"

Mrs Peaton pours us the deliciously scenting Darjeeling tea in my favourite Wedgewood cups. I surely missed those in my rented apartment over Hopewell's bookshop.

"That's what I wanted to discuss with you in private, Mrs Lynch."

My eyes grow wide with trepidation. If she's going to leave me now, I'm going to collapse on the spot. Jasper seems to sense my distress and firmly places his snout on my shoe.

"Are you...?"

"No, no, don't worry. I've met someone." Mrs Peaton round face turns crimson and my heart skips a beat. *She couldn't have found love again?* But then the next gulf of fear washes over me. Then she will certainly leave me.

"Who is it?" I blurt out. "Someone I know?"

Mrs Peaton dips her head as if ashamed. Why would anyone be ashamed of love, the most precious of human feelings?

"It is, Mrs Lynch, it is..." She hesitates, looks out of the freshly washed windows with the white lace curtains. "It is Bernie Craig, your gardener."

"Bernie?" It takes me a minute to visualize the stout, ruddy, short-legged Bernie, who's as silent as the elves, as Mrs Peaton's beau, but then the penny drops.

"Of course!" I cry out, "I had totally forgotten he's a widower with two grown sons. Oh, I'm so happy for you."

Mrs Peaton looks as if a thirty-pound sack of flour is taken off her shoulder.

"Really?" Her sweet face with the light eyes gleam with pleasure, "I wasn't sure how you would take it. I wanted your approval first and nothing's going to change. We're not starting a family at our age." She points to her greying hair, "and we would just like to keep looking after Honeydew Mansion for you as we've done for years."

While I'm feeling relieved of my own burden, my mind races.

"You'll both stay at the cottage, of course. It hasn't been used for ages, but I'm sure Bernie can do it up nicely for you both."

"Oh, we'd hoped you'd say that, Mrs Lynch, but it's really no trouble for me to keep living in the house and if you'd be in London for a while it might actually be safer to have someone in the big house."

"When were you planning on getting married?"

"Well, now you consent to it, we can start planning, can't we? But really, we are in no rush. Though Bernie and I enjoy each other's company, he's quite content in his house in Landdulton and I'm happy where I am."

"Well, just make sure you invite me to the wedding!"

"Of course. I'd love for you to be my witness, if you would, Mrs Lynch!"

"That would be marvellous! Oh, you've certainly made my day, Mrs Peaton! Or should I call you Mrs Craig now?"

"Mrs Peaton for you always, Ma'am."

My own melancholia temporarily melts away at this blissful announcement of new love found at a mature age.

At that moment the door knocker comes down twice.

"Who can that be?" I wonder aloud. Mrs Peaton's deliveries are always brought to the back door and we're not expecting visitors. I just felt perked up enough to take Jasper for his walk.

"I'll have a look." Mrs Peaton puts her teacup down and takes off her apron.

Seconds later I'm surprised to hear Doctor Rule's familiar voice asking if I'm home. My GP's arrival instantly alarms me something is wrong with Finley or Anna. Or God forbid, Catherine.

"Imogene!" The jovial Ed Rule comes towards me and grabs both my hands. No sign of a calamity there.

"Ed? What brings you here?" I smile in return, always pleased to see my white-haired doctor who is also my friend and with whom I shared so much when Thaddeus fell ill.

"I passed by from seeing a patient and I have a spare hour. I know you usually go for your morning walk with Jasper and the weather is so inviting. I was wondering if I could accompany you on your walk?"

I raise one eyebrow. This is very un-Doctor Rule-like, also not speaking in short, staccato sentences and I feel I'm putting up my investigation cap, but I say nothing.

"Absolutely. I was just on my way out."

Jasper is wriggling his roly-poly body in delight. He likes the doctor, but he likes rushing along the shoreline even more.

As soon as we're out of earshot from the house, I fire my question. "What is this about, Ed? Let the cat out of the bag."

"There's no sugar-coating with you, Imogene, is there?"

"No there isn't." I say with a little laugh.

"I'm worried about you."

As if he's the investigator now, he doesn't say more, which forces me to ask.

"What about?"

"Your mental well-being. After the first rough and tumble of mourning, grief becomes more of a cyclic affair. As Thaddeus passed away last year's spring, this spring is going to be the hardest for you. You've come full circle, so to say. That's what you are experiencing now."

I'm listening intently to his words. I hadn't thought of grief as a cycle myself, but it makes sense. It is as if my body remembers that a year of day after day without my benedict has passed.

"So that's it?" I'm thinking aloud, my eyes watching Jasper splash through the cold water as if he's a pup all over again.

"Yes, that's it, Imogene."

"Well, I'll just have to grasp the nettle and live with it. What choice do I have?"

"Distraction. New surroundings."

I can't help but laugh out loud.

"You must have been talking with Cousin Catherine, Ed."

He shrugs his shoulder, halts in the sand, and looks at me squarely. The honey-brown eyes probing me.

"What if I have?"

I stop as well. Take in my surroundings. Feel the heaviness of my heart, the emptiness, the pain.

"But Cairo, Ed? For sure not Cairo?

"Yes Cairo, Imogene. London holds memories for you as well. You need to go where you have no memories. That's why in a way Dartmond worked for you last year. But now go for a vacation, enjoy yourself, free yourself, so to say."

"But I can't, Ed. I can't leave Mrs Peaton look after the house on her own again. And what about Jasper?"

The doctor follows my eyes and watches Jasper snapping at the foamy waves.

"Jasper goes where you go, Imogene. Don't worry about him."

"But he's old." I feel like running out of options.

"They have veterinarians in Egypt. And also on the ship."

"How do you know that?" I become suspicious.

"I didn't. Catherine found out."

I sigh, call Jasper to my side who leaves the shoreline reluctantly.

"You two seem to have it all mapped out for me."

Now it's the doctor's time to sigh.

"I know it's a big step for you, Imogene. But you told me you used to travel with your parents before you married, and you and Thaddeus had an extended honeymoon in Italy."

Flashes of memories flood back to me, scents, sounds, and colours. Marrakech, New York, Biarritz, Nice. And of course, Florence, Rome, Venice ... Hanging onto Thaddeus's arm in my white silk dress with matching hat. A young bride, giddy with love.

Could I? Would I?

"Let me sleep on it." My voice is husky, emotional.

"That's all I'm asking from you at this point, my friend and patient. And feel free to talk with Julietta. Being from Greece, my wife has travelled to Egypt quite often. She can tell you what it's like if you fear Catherine only paints too pretty a picture."

"I will do that." I say, "And thank you, Ed. Catherine would never have persuaded me, but you..."

That night, when I'm lying in my bed, feeling the cold place next to me, my mind starts roaming my wardrobe, what to wear, what to purchase in London. On our way to the Orient.

I'm going to Cairo.

ABOUT THE AUTHOR

"Ever since I could hold a pen, I've written poems and stories and I'll write till my dying day."

Historical fiction author Hannah Byron's crib stood near the Seine in Paris, but she was raised in the south of Holland by Anglo-Dutch parents. In her bestselling WW2 historical fiction series, The Resistance Girl Series, Hannah's heroines also traipse from one European country to the next, very much like their creator.

Now a retired university lecturer and translator, the European traveler and avid researcher is about to cross a new border and settle down south of Dublin.

What started as curiosity about her family's connection to D-Day, evolved into an out-of-controlish study into WW2 history. To blame, or thank, must be Uncle Tom Naylor. If he'd not landed on the beaches of Normandy and helped liberate Holland, her British mother would never have met her Dutch Dad after the war.

Strong women are at the core of her clean and wholesome romance novels. Every book is a tribute to the generation that started the women's lib movement, got dirty in overalls, flew planes, and did intelligence work. Today's girl bosses can but stand on the shoulders of these amazons.

Side-by-side with their male counterparts, Byron's heroines fight for freedom, equality and... love.

In December 2022, Byron launches her first Historical Mysteries. *The Mrs Imogene Lynch Series* stars the kind but opinionated Victorian widow of Constable Thaddeus Lynch.

ALSO BY HANNAH BYRON

The Resistance Girl Series

In Picardy's Fields

The Diamond Courier

The Parisian Spy

The Norwegian Assassin

The Highland Raven

The Crystal Butterfly (preorder)

The Agnès Duet

Miss Agnes

Doctor Agnes

The Mrs Imogene Lynch Series

The Unsolved Case of the Secret Christmas Baby

The Peculiar Vanishing Act of Mr Ralph Herriot (preorder)

Made in the USA
Middletown, DE
13 December 2022

18484747R00139